"I'm not ready to become part of a couple now," Genie said, not adding: the invisible part.

The annoyance on Danny's face changed to an expression of perplexity. "Yesterday, you gave yourself to me. *All* of yourself, I could feel it."

"Yes."

"Then why?"

She sighed. "We're both at the beginning of our careers, and each of us needs to do our work."

"You could help me. Living with you, Genie love, I'd be constantly inspired."

Genie shook her head. She didn't know how to make him understand. Danny's enthusiasm, his love of life, his intense vitality made him the most exciting man she'd ever been with. Her body loved him. But she felt his intensity was also dangerous to her—that he'd want to devour her. She couldn't live with a man who jeopardized her life's goals.

Danny looked at her, the glowing hair, the high planes of her cheekbones, the dark eyes. She was myriad, faceted like a finely cut gemstone. The woman who'd given herself to him, given herself for the first time, but in full ardor, was now a cool princess who asked to be left alone. Her strange independence excited and challenged him. He'd try later. He'd make her vulnerable to him and in time he would possess her completely. . . .

Books by Johanna Kingsley:

SCENTS
FACES

FACES

Johanna Kingsley

BANTAM BOOKS
TORONTO · NEW YORK · LONDON · SYDNEY · AUCKLAND

FACES

A Bantam Book / April 1987

Grateful acknowledgment is made for permission to reprint lines
from "The Love Song of J. Alfred Prufrock" by T.S. Eliot found in
Collected Poems 1909–1962 by T.S. Eliot, copyright 1936 by
Harcourt Brace Jovanovich, Inc., copyright © 1963, 1964 by T.S.
Eliot. Reprinted by permission of Harcourt Brace Jovanovich, Inc.
and Faber and Faber Publishers.

ISBN 0-553-25418-9

Published simultaneously in the United States and Canada

PRINTED IN THE UNITED STATES OF AMERICA

KR   0 9 8 7 6 5 4 3 2 1

ACKNOWLEDGMENT

Books, like people, are the result of conception, labor, and issue. Without the skilled and loving assistance of my editor, Jeanne Bernkopf, through all the time when it was taking shape, this novel would not have come into being.

J.K.

PROLOGUE

"**M**ake me beautiful."

Dr. Eugenia Sareyov studied the woman sitting opposite her. A senator's wife, fine-boned with a fair complexion, the type least likely to retain scars. She was holding herself tall and straight in her Calvin Klein silk, legs crossed at the knees, her left foot flexing up and down in quick jerks. "My husband . . ." she began, and caught her lower lip between her teeth. "I've got to get him back," she blurted, "or at least get even."

"You're a very attractive woman, Mrs. Barett," the doctor told her.

"A face lift. Please. I'll pay anything. Make me stunning!"

"You don't need one. The effects of a face lift would be barely noticeable," Genie Sareyov said. "You'd simply look well-rested."

"That can't be all!"

"That's all."

"I'm forty-two, going on eighty-three!" A note of hysteria entered Evelyn Barett's voice. "You've got to *do* something!"

Genie's practiced eye took in the features and contours. No obvious imperfection to be excised or surgically molded. "I'd be taking advantage of your present state if I agreed to operate. Wherever the problem lies, it's not with your physical

3

appearance." Why did people think they could be changed from the outside in?

"Who are you to tell me that?" Evelyn Barett pitched forward in the chair, her voice edged now with malice. "You must be about my age—but look at you. You're beautiful and you've got everything . . ."

"Hold on. Why compare yourself to anyone else? We're talking about you."

The fight went out of her body, but Evelyn still struggled verbally. "I can afford it. You're the best. You're one of us, you belong in the same crowd. You've got no business refusing me," she shrilled. "I'll go somewhere else."

"I can't stop you, and I'm sure you'll find someone willing to take your money. But it *is* my business. I'm a doctor, not a body mechanic. Whatever reputation I have comes from knowing how to operate, and when, and when not to." Genie could feel the anger pressing against her throat. Her knuckles were white on her clenched fists. She took a deep breath and unclasped her hands. The woman came for help, not a lecture.

"I'm sorry," Genie started again. "I don't think a plastic surgeon can do anything for you."

"There are plenty of other surgeons."

Her anger flared up again, beyond her usual control. "Go to them. I'm not a knife for hire."

"I wanted magic," Evelyn Barett said softly. "I hoped you'd wave a wand and make me beautiful. Happy again."

Genie recognized the familiar hope. "Like Cinderella. If I could do that, I wouldn't need a knife." She stood up. "And I'd be in a different profession."

She escorted her patient to the door and returned slowly to her desk. She should have canceled this afternoon's appointments, she thought. Tomorrow's operation preyed on her mind, upsetting her professional poise.

Evelyn Barett had expected her to operate on dreams. But so had countless others over the years; she'd overreacted. Must calm down, Genie told herself.

Tomorrow she would invade her own dream. Right now she had patients to take care of.

Her next one came in through the sliding panel, a special device constructed for the protection of Genie's star and superstar clients, who used the secret entrance and the maze leading up to it from the basement garage to escape from the media hounds following them in close pursuit.

Chet Amor walked into the office with a swagger that had become part of his gait as the leading man of television's most popular soap. Amor's face in any magazine or newspaper didn't need a caption to identify it. At his side was his lover of ten years, Genie's patient.

John Darwin had undergone a sex-change operation six weeks earlier, after nearly eighteen months of hormone treatment. The steroids had softened his features, encouraged breast development, and reduced body hair. Surgery had replaced the penis with a vagina. Now, as Jane, she came to discuss the plastic surgery that would complete her transformation.

"I've become a woman and I'm very happy," she told the doctor, "but I'd like to be an *attractive* woman."

Genie studied the face, looked down at the chest. The breasts were slight, like a young girl's.

Jane Darwin smiled. "Not that. I don't want implants. No foreign substances in my body—the steroids were bad enough. I figure it's okay to look like a model, and it means I can go topless if the style ever comes back. The problem, doctor, is my nose."

Genie agreed, but asked cautiously, "Why do you want it changed now? It's the same nose you always had."

"But I'm not the same person I was. I didn't like myself physically, and as long as I was a man I didn't think about improving my looks. But I'm a woman now, and with a thinner nose, less fleshy here, on the tip, my face would be in proportion."

"Yes," Genie said. She glanced at Chet Amor. "The two of you have discussed this, I take it?"

Jane nodded. "Yes. Chet supports me. As far back as I can remember, I felt I was a girl misplaced in a boy's body. Of course I want to please Chet, but not through a disguise. At thirty, I finally look like me."

"I loved John," Chet broke in. "When he decided for the sex change, I didn't want him to do it at first."

"Why not?" Genie asked.

He shrugged. "Selfish, I guess. I wanted him to remain the way he was when we met. He was a kid then, looked up to me, made me feel important. I wanted his 'secret' to be something that just the two of us knew about. I suppose I was afraid of it.

"We went to therapy together. I realized I'd been needing *his* insecurity to protect me from facing my own. I loved John," he repeated, "but maybe I love Jane even more." He gave Jane a wink and touched her wrist with his fingertips.

"Will you come next door, please?" Genie said to her patient. "I'll examine you. Then I'll send you to a medical photographer. When would you like to schedule the operation?"

Jane clapped her hands. "Tomorrow!"

A shadow passed over Genie's face as she led the way to the examining room. "That's not possible," she said. "How about two weeks from today?"

"Thank you, doctor. You're the answer to my prayers."

Between consultations, Genie made phone calls. Most of them concerned the next morning's surgery—calls to the radiology lab, the anesthesiologist, the assisting surgeon, the chief nurse on her patient's floor—though Genie knew, even while she phoned, that the calls were superfluous, that she was checking and double-checking in response to her own anxiety.

Then she turned back to her patients in the cosmetic wing of the clinic. She listened to the problems they brought to her, reviewed charts and medical histories, answered their questions, did a post-op examination of an aging scriptwriter who'd had a face lift, another of a young entertainer whose ears she'd recently reduced and sculpted.

Sculpted, she thought wryly, as she checked the newly healed sutures. "You're doing fine," she told the singer. "Right on schedule."

As she watched him leave, Genie had an image of the clinic's founder. Nicknamed "the Knife," Max Bonner would have refused even to consult with most of the people who came to Genie's office. He was the one who'd called the elective surgery wing a "fix-it shop" when she'd first proposed it, and had shouted that he was "no fucking mechanic." Later, when the wing was officially opened, he'd derided it as a "temple of vanity." Max had been a surgeon, first and last—no "sculptor" either. Plastic surgery meant only one thing to him, and that was reconstruction. His enemy had been deformity, and his life a battle to vanquish it. If Max were here, Genie thought, he'd be scrubbing with me tomorrow.

* * *

She rushed through her last consultation of the day, agreeing to perform a lipectomy on the plump thighs of a former actress. Any other day she would have made the thigh reduction conditional on the woman's first shedding at least thirty pounds. But that would mean prolonging the consultation, and Genie had to get away. She couldn't breathe in the air of her office.

She left abruptly, merely calling out good-bye to her nurse. She ran out to her Ferrari, jumped in, and kept the accelerator pressed down to the floor. Usually Genie didn't take advantage of her M.D. license plate, but this evening she tore down the Monterey Peninsula as though pursued by fates.

She pulled up into her driveway and snapped off the engine, leaving the car choking in protest. She jogged into the house, pulling at her clothes as she entered. She threw them on a chair in her bedroom and grabbed her bathing suit, stepping into it as she slid open the glass doors leading to the pool.

Sixty feet long, heated to eighty-two degrees throughout the year, her pool was an extravagance she considered necessary. Every morning or evening—both, when she could manage it—Genie swam vigorous laps, relaxing her mind in the steady rhythm of her body.

This evening, relaxation wouldn't come. She swam for twenty minutes, then twenty more. Another ten. She went up to the house, turbaned her hair in a lilac towel, and put on a terry bathrobe.

In the kitchen, she opened and closed the refrigerator several times, finding nothing to tempt her. The house had a brooding emptiness about it. Though she'd lived alone for many—for most—of her adult years, tonight the absence of one person filled all the rooms. She would see him in the morning, early, on the operating table, and until then there was nothing to do but go to bed.

She dozed fitfully, waking often to images that frightened her out of sleep, a series of Halloween masks fusing with the skin of her patient's face when she tried to remove them surgically.

At four-thirty in the morning Genie got up. She could smell the sourness of her own nervous perspiration and stripped back the sheets. Naked, Genie slid open the doors, switched on the underwater lights, and dived into the pool.

At six, in her white surgeon's gown, Dr. Genie Sareyov was in the clinic, in the old building where she and Max Bonner had operated on veterans. They'd been understaffed then, lacking essential equipment and supplies, especially blood.

Now, the clinic had everything: stores of blood that included the rarest types, a highly qualified staff, the most sophisticated instruments available, the latest in diagnostic computers.

Genie checked the patient's chart again. She reviewed her instructions to each member of the team that would be assisting her. But her anxiousness persisted, a sense that she'd overlooked something crucial. She brought out the medical photographs, in life size and magnification, and pored over them for the third time that morning.

At a quarter to seven she was going over the data on the new display system one last time, the high-resolution images of digital slices made from the patient's head. With each image she studied, she went down a mental checklist of the procedures she would follow, of complications that were even vaguely possible.

In an hour and a half—less—she'd be performing the operation she'd dreamed of hundreds of times, had pictured herself doing since she'd started medical school. Even earlier than that, not knowing how it was done, she'd had the dream of restoring that particular face, freeing it from its disfigurement.

She turned off the scanner. The minute hand was nearly at twelve. Seven A.M. Any moment now, the nurse would be administering Demerol to put the patient into a twilight consciousness before wheeling him to the operating room. . . .

Suddenly Genie was sure of nothing. She had to get to him right away. She pushed open the door of the computer room and rushed down the corridor to the man whose life had shaped her own.

PART I

PART I

1

1957

Snow was still falling, as it had been since Evgenia Sareyov woke up in the morning, and even on Leningrad's main avenue the large drifts turned walking into a battle. Sharp gusts tore at her face as Genia worked her way home from ballet school, two hours earlier than usual. In late January, daylight lasted only a short time. It was fading already and despite her heavy overcoat Genia was chilly. She lowered her lashes, tipped with frost. Large white flakes landed on her sleeve and she watched them etch a moment's decal against the dark blue wool, then vanish. She put out her tongue to taste the cold and shivered. She'd been expelled; what would her father do?

From Nevsky Prospekt she took her usual shortcut to the great square. Behind a shifting veil of snow, the Winter Palace was a muted warm green, the color of unripe blueberries.

Near the Admiralty, boys were building a large snowman, hatless despite the cold. Their long hair was worn in last year's "Tarzan look," a style that had spread among Soviet youth after the American movie came to Moscow. Now, more than a year later, the fad was out-of-date, but the boys showed off their daring in the square as they put the finishing touches on their snowman. At school, Genia and her friends made fun of the "Tarzaniks," but here she was alone and afraid of them.

She tried to hurry, hoping the snowflakes would settle long enough on her overcoat to make her invisible. But the boys

11

caught sight of her, a pretty girl with cherry cheeks and generous mouth, and they called out, "Jane! Jane!"

She slid her boots one in front of the other as though they were small skis and turned her head away from them. Her father called such people "malingerers" or "parasites."

He would be angry with her, Genia was sure, probably furious, and her mother would do nothing to calm him, even if she were home. Her mother was the one who insisted on culture for her children.

Genia had never been in the least interested in ballet, though her parents had wanted her to go to the Kirov— probably because of its prestige. But she was not qualified for ballet school of any kind, let alone the best in the world. Even a minor school like her own had been reluctant to take her last year, at the advanced age of eleven. She guessed how much pressure her father must have put on people to get her accepted. And now she was thrown out!

Genia walked slowly, her boots disappearing under the snow. A clod. Teacher Kondrashin had shouted at her: "Your feet, they are glued to the ground. Pick them up. Up!"

He was temperamental, an artist, with a wild mane of hair and a long pointed nose that made him look like a pencil, *karandash*. That's what his pupils called him behind his back, though Genia was fond of him. She knew he was right about her dancing ability. "Only on the moon," he'd sputtered, "could you be a dancer—where there is no gravity."

Today she'd tripped over the feet of the girl beside her and fallen in such a way that the line of girls tumbled over each other like dominoes. For Kondrashin, that was it. "Let them do with me what they will!" he exploded. "I cannot teach an elephant to dance. Evgenia Giorgovna, out with you! Out of my sight, now!"

Unless she could make up a story to protect him, Teacher Kondrashin might be in serious trouble. Her father had taken severe measures against people who displeased him before. Poor Pencil, she thought.

"Jane!" she heard again faintly and, confident that she was now at a safe distance from the boys, Genia turned back to look at them.

They were standing beside their snowman, and when they saw her watching, they waved. To her horror, Genia could see the snowman waving too. It had become alive, a creature formed of ice and snow.

Genia gasped, tried to run, and fell headlong into the snow. She pushed herself up with her hands. Her face was burning with cold, her wrists were raw and freezing where the snow came in between her sleeves and her gloves. She was sure they were laughing at her, and she moved as quickly as she could, shuffling one foot after another, spurred by fear.

The snowman was her father.

Genia had been born in 1944, in the wake of the longest and most devastating siege the world had known. The Siege of Leningrad had lasted for nine hundred days. Hitler's armies had formed a blockade, sealing off the city from all supplies. Over a million people had died in the stranglehold, of starvation, bullets, disease, and the killing cold. Old people and the very young froze to death. Sleds so tiny they could have been meant for dolls were constructed to pull dead babies through frozen streets to the overcrowded cemeteries.

Leningrad itself might have fallen to the Nazis, if not for a trickle of food, ammunition, and medicine carried into the city on a thin lifeline. That was the route across Lake Ladoga—by boat or barge in summer, by truck across the hard ice in winter. Known as "the road of life," it was there that Genia's father had met his terrible destiny.

The cold had shredded and ripped at his face, tearing off extremities, branding him with the mutilations of frostbite.

It would have been easier if he'd died, Genia sometimes thought. Then she would have been free to imagine him, and she could have made him up to look like a normal father. But he had survived and been proclaimed a hero for his valor in fighting and for his endurance through torture. After the war, he had received a high-level Party position as sinecure.

Genia had never seen a picture of him before the siege, and she didn't remember his face from the time when she was a baby. Probably she'd thought that all people, or fathers, looked like that. Maybe she didn't notice that he had a gaping hole where a nose should be, or that his ear was missing, or that his skin was glazed in patches. But now she was grown, she would be thirteen in May, and sometimes when she looked at him she wished he'd been killed on Lake Ladoga. Her thoughts frightened her and she kept them to herself, telling no one about them, not even her brother.

Her father had always been good to her, she told herself. He

was clever and important, a hero of the country—everybody
knew that. She'd willed herself to love him years earlier, but
she dreaded having him touch her.

He never tried to touch their mother, Genia observed, and
she wondered about it. Natalya Leonova was beautiful, with a
complexion so clear it seemed to be lighted from within.
Maybe her father was afraid that his touch would leave an ugly
mark on the silken skin.

Genia tried not to think like that. She couldn't remember
when she had first seen how ugly he was, and she tried
convincing herself that others saw him differently, that it was
her own wickedness that made her see him as she did.

But one day in school, when she'd been about eight and a
half, Genia had overheard two little girls talking about him.
They giggled and chanted, "Comrade Sareyov is the Monster."

Genia had wanted to jump on them, scream at them,
denounce them. But in the end all she did was cry by herself,
in frustration and helplessness. She knew that they were right,
and that she'd been seeing her father as he really was all along.
Loving to her, but a monstrosity, like a living snowman.

The streetlamps were on as she came toward her house,
spotlighting thick circles and spirals of dancing snow. To
Genia, there was nothing beautiful in the sight. For the last
hundred steps or so, she'd felt so cold she thought her blood
would become ice if she stood still for only a moment. As long
as I keep moving, she told herself, all the cells in me will be
shaken around and won't freeze.

She pictured the cells as infinitesimally small worlds where
the tiniest creatures lived. It was a fantasy she'd had for years.
She, Genia, was their universe, and she could never run down
or they would die.

A few more minutes and she'd be home. Home: the samovar
lighted in the sitting room, Aunt Katya coming in with a plate
of sweet rolls and filling Genia's glass with tea. Then Genia
would drink the hot, strong liquid through a lump of sugar she
held against her teeth with her tongue. After the tea, Aunt
Katya would draw a bath. Katya wasn't an aunt, not even a
relative of any kind, but everyone at home called her
tetyuschka, Aunty, as people used to in the old days.

When Genia came up the steps and pulled open the heavy
polished door, she had a premonition of doom. Everything was

too still; she could feel a pall in the air. Did they know already that her career as a ballerina had been squashed under the weightiness of a baby elephant? She stood in the hallway, not daring to announce her arrival.

Bustling in from the sitting room, her face imprinted with lines of worry, Aunt Katya embraced the girl quickly and told her to go upstairs to wait for her father.

"But I'm cold, *tetyuschka!*" Genia protested.

"I'll bring you a glass of tea. Upstairs now, my poor child." She made quick shooing motions with her hands.

Genia left her boots by the door and walked up in stocking feet. Her "room" was an area partitioned off from her brother's in what had once been an Imperial drawing room in the days of Catherine the Great. As a mark of privilege, because he was a Party secretary and an official in the Ministry of Trade, Giorgi and his family had been assigned an apartment in the small baroque palace designed in the style of Rastrelli, architect of the Winter Palace. During the Bolshevik Revolution, the Italianate building had become state property, when it had been divided up into apartments.

The children had shared the large drawing room with its domed, embossed ceiling until Dmitri entered secondary school. Then a wooden partition had been put in to separate them, providing some privacy for each, though sound and light passed overhead in the space above the wall below the dome.

Genia opened the door and heard an unfamiliar sound coming from her brother's partition. After a moment or two she placed it. The sound was unfamiliar only because it was coming from him. Dmitri was crying.

Alarmed, she knocked gently against the wall, then more strongly when he didn't respond. She called out to him, but his only answer was sudden silence. After a few minutes the crying began again, more faintly than before, as though it were being muffled.

Genia sat down on her bed, still in her overcoat. She didn't know what to make of it. Why should her brother be so distressed? He'd always known that she hated ballet school.

She felt the presence of her father in the door frame. She looked up and met his stare. Grotesque and terrible, Giorgi Sareyov stood motionless. His skin shone like pitted rubber, his left eye twitched. Under the dark cavity in the center of his face, his open mouth seemed like another mutilation.

He let out a gasp as he hobbled into the room. Genia drew

back on the bed, hugging herself in her coat. She focused on his neck.

"She's gone, my beauty." His words were low and sad. His voice didn't frighten her.

"Who?"

"Natasha. Natasha. Natalya Leonova."

"Mother? Where?"

"Gone. Gone." The left eye stopped twitching as tears spilled over onto his cheeks. He came to the bed and sat down at its end. Genia hugged herself tighter.

"Natasha," he repeated. "Your mother, yes. My wife, the famous whore Natasha. My *former* wife. Slut."

Aunt Katya came in with the tea and set down the tray on the small round table. She knelt in front of Genia. "My poor orphan!" she cried. "Your mama's left us!"

Genia looked down at her. What did her mother have to do with her expulsion from ballet school?

Aunt Katya crossed herself, surreptitiously so Giorgi wouldn't notice, but he was crying, not looking at her. "She packed her bags and made off," Katya wailed. "Just like that. She ran away with Konstantin Yasnikoff. The disgrace! The pity! My poor lamb!"

"The actor?" He was one of her mother's circle of friends, the theater people who came to the house on Wednesday evenings. Her father always went up to his room when they arrived, saying that theater was "only for the frivolous." "You mean Kostya?" asked Genia.

"The very same, the scoundrel. Handsome, to be sure, and talented from what one hears, but what a ruffian . . ."

"Enough rubbish," said Giorgi. "Leave me to talk with my daughter alone."

"Poor darling little orphan," Katya murmured as she was getting up. Genia wanted her to stay, not to leave her alone with her father.

Katya walked out shaking her head and muttering softly.

"So," Giorgi said in a bitter voice, as though talking to an adult. "Now you know. I have been left. Deserted. For an actor!"

Genia felt hot in her coat, but she didn't dare take it off. She didn't dare move. Everything was so strange. She believed it and didn't believe it at the same time. Her mother was often out or away. Surely she'd be back by evening?

Genia waited. Her father sobbed, then cursed with a string

of words she didn't understand, then fell into silence. After a long time, he spoke to her again, in a voice like the sad music of wind roaming through an empty house.

"We were very much in love once. She made up songs about me, how big and handsome I was. She was always giving me something—kisses, flowers, pretty little words written on scraps of paper or birch." He drew a deep breath, which grated in his throat. "We lived in peace. In happiness. Dmitri was born. Then came the war, the barricades. I had to leave and she couldn't come with me . . ." He stared out at something Genia couldn't see, and shuddered.

"When I came back . . . like this"—he opened his palms and raised his face upward—"she couldn't bear to look at me. She was disgusted. Her eyes were mirrors to my ugliness."

His unhappiness filled the room, and Genia felt it as she breathed. She reached out and touched her father's arm, not looking at his face. He'd been handsome once, he said. He'd never told her that; neither had her mother.

"The old photographs were still here when I came back. I tore them up, all of them."

"Why?" she asked, wishing he'd saved at least one.

"You can't understand, Genia. I was jealous. Jealous of *him*, her handsome lover, the one who'd taken all her love with him and lost it.

"Yes," he repeated. "I was jealous. And then I began to hate her."

He turned toward his daughter and took her hand. The stubs of his fingers were thick, like parsnips. When she was smaller, she used to wonder why they didn't grow. She'd asked him once, but he'd simply stared, without answering.

"Genia! She's gone!"

A wave of nausea rose up, and she closed her eyes. The nausea passed, and was followed by a wave of fear.

"The whore!"

Her mother had left her. Disappeared as though dead, but it was worse. She'd *wanted* to go away.

"Did she . . . did she leave anything for me?"

"What do you mean?" he asked sternly. "What kind of thing?"

"I don't know. A note? A letter? You know, *something*," she pleaded.

"No," he said curtly. "*Nichevo niet*." He looked at her

frightened face, held her eyes for a moment, and repeated with finality: "Nothing."

She stared at his missing ear, hating him for his deformity, for driving her mother away, for saying that she'd left nothing. Then Genia realized she was alone with him now, and began to sob.

2

After his wife left, Giorgi began each day with vodka. Evenings, he went out alone and came back to the house late, drunk and morose. His bouts of self-pity sometimes woke the children and they'd creep down to look at him, seated at the kitchen table, his parsnip fingers rooted to the vodka bottle. They could see the tracks of his tears on the unshaven cheeks, over the shiny dead patches and through the hairs sprouting from sections of living skin.

When he caught them watching, Giorgi let out a shout and began cursing, as they hurried away to a new cover. He cursed them for stealing their mother's love from him, or conversely, for being such troublemakers that they had forced her to go away.

Dmitri and Genia listened from their new hiding place, holding hands tightly, and their father's accusations veered to other targets as he cursed his wife, the Germans, the siege, his wife again, the unending cold of Lake Ladoga. If they stayed long enough, they usually heard him sob for many minutes without speaking, and then in a low, breaking voice repeat over and over again: "This face, my face."

Genia understood that her mother had left them because of that face. Her father's ugliness had destroyed their family.

But it made no sense. He'd always looked like that. Why should she leave now?

And besides, the mutilation was a sign of his bravery. It made him a hero. Because of what happened in the war, they were all living in this grand apartment, a palace compared to the homes of most of Genia's schoolmates. Because of the war, too, Giorgi Sareyov held an important government position. Though the fact that he worked at home, Genia remembered, was because of his face. He didn't want, or wasn't permitted, to work in a public place where others could see him.

He went out at night now, screened by darkness, and always alone. By day he was locked in his study, and only silence emanated from his room.

In late February, Genia and Dmitri were returning upstairs after watching their father's rage and self-pity for more than an hour. As they entered Dmitri's partition, Genia asked: "Do you think Father is really two people?"

"More than that," Dmitri said. "He's a mess of people."

"No, that isn't what I mean." She crawled into bed with her brother, as they used to do when they were little. "I mean, does he have two sides? Good and ugly, quiet and angry?"

"Just drunk and not so drunk," Dmitri said sharply.

Aunt Katya, hearing them, had come into the room and whispered that Genia was to go to her own bed. She had school tomorrow and would be dead on her feet if she didn't get back to sleep immediately.

With Katya's arm around her, Genia shuffled back to her partition. When Katya kissed her good night, Genia asked: "Do you think my father is a good man or a bad one?"

"What a question!" Katya drew back and crossed herself quickly. "He's your father."

"I know that," Genia answered impatiently. It was hopeless trying to talk to Katya now that she felt nearly grown. Genia was aware that the older woman was kind and loving, and that she herself had loved Katya very much when she was a child. But now, whatever Katya said sounded so simple!

It was because of God, Genia decided. Katya was a true believer in the old Orthodox religion, and Genia was a Soviet girl, a member of the Pioneers, who'd learned that religion was a kind of drug that had dulled people's minds in the days before Lenin. Since then, people had been shown the way to belief in man, progress, and the ultimate goal of Communism.

"Sleep well, dear lamb," Katya said.

"And my mother," Genia insisted. "Is she good or bad?"

She heard the sharp intake of Katya's breath. "Your mother was a beautiful woman, and loved you dearly."

Katya walked quickly out of the room, leaving Genia to ponder her use of the past tense. Did that mean her mother was dead?

After a few minutes, lying in the dark, Genia couldn't stand the shriek of questions whistling through her brain. Taking care to make no sound, she left her bed again and went back to Dmitri's.

He might have been sleeping. He was lying on his back when she pulled at the blankets, and he moved toward the right to give her more room. When she was in the bed with the blankets pulled over her, Dmitri gave her a loose hug, almost an absentminded embrace from out of sleep.

"Where's our mother?" she whispered urgently. "Where did she go?"

He didn't answer for a moment, and his hold slackened. "Somewhere beautiful," he said, no hint of drowsiness in his voice.

"Is she . . . ?" Genia couldn't bring herself to say it; instead, she asked: "Is she all right?"

Again, he let a moment go by. "I don't know."

Genia felt confused. More than that, frightened. Dmitri had been so close to their mother, much closer than she had been. He was older, he had to know something.

"Why didn't she leave a note?"

"I don't know!" He sounded impatient.

"You're not going away, are you?"

No answer.

Genia sat up and turned on the light. "You can't! Ever!"

He gave a weak smile. "All right."

"Do you think she'll be back?"

He groaned and turned on his side away from her. He didn't speak to her again, and after a few minutes Genia got up.

She didn't sleep for the rest of the night. Dmitri's silence, his coldness, was the worst of anything that had happened. Or maybe it was that he'd been her last hope, last anchor, and now he, too, had slipped away from her. The third abandonment was the worst. In the dark room, her eyes open, Genia felt she'd come to the edge of the world and had fallen off into everlasting night.

By morning she had decided to leave childhood behind. She would depend on no one but herself, and perhaps the members of her Pioneer group. She would cut off ties with her family and enter into the community of peers. She would never again go into her brother's bed.

Dmitri was fifteen and loved his mother passionately. The sun had risen and set with her and now the world had become bleak, so desolate that he couldn't help crying every night, though he cried soundlessly and often without tears. Dmitri loved his sister too, but she was a child and her vulnerability terrified him. He closed himself off from everyone, including Genia.

Nearly every moment that she wasn't in school, Genia spent with the Pioneers. In March they began building a nursery for young children. Together with members of the Komsomol, the Communist Youth Organization, they mixed concrete, poured it into molds to harden, and then fitted the blocks in place. The work was demanding, physically exhausting, and Genia was the hardest worker of all.

Dmitri's energies went into studies, mainly, though he too was often away from home. Genia didn't ask, and Dmitri didn't tell her where he went.

Katya worried about the children and fussed over them as though they were incapable of doing anything themselves. This irritated them both, and they were often abrupt with her. But Katya forgave them, or else didn't notice their rudeness. She felt it was her duty, to God and to them, to become their mother. Her own children, both boys, had died of starvation in the siege, and her husband had been murdered for the sake of a small loaf of bread he'd been carrying under his arm. To Katya it seemed that God was righting the balance, giving her a man and two orphans to care for.

Giorgi ignored her and the children. For six weeks he lived in a sea of alcohol, riding its turbulence and calm, hoping it would drown him. But then, slowly, he began to notice that life went on and he remembered, though still hazily, that he was a father.

He spoke gently to Genia when he saw her, and asked questions about what she was doing. She talked of the Pioneers mainly, and told him what she was studying in school.

The atmosphere was changing at home. Dmitri was still aloof and Aunt Katya remained overly solicitous, but Genia was no longer frightened of her father. She began to relax in his presence, and she could feel some of his old warmth coming back. He didn't rage at night anymore, and he limited his breakfast vodka to one or two glasses only. Exactly two months after her mother's flight, on a blustery March 27, Genia came home in the evening after several hours of strenuous work at the nursery site. She'd been sweating as she mixed and lifted the concrete, but on the way home her perspiration dried inside her clothing and she was shivering. She ran the last part of the way, already feeling the hot tea lacing her tongue. But when she opened the door, Aunt Katya didn't rush to meet her as she always did, clucking with concern at her dusty hair and disheveled clothes.

Curious, Genia went looking for Aunt Katya and found her in the kitchen polishing the silver that had belonged to Natasha's mother, an elaborate set made in England. Genia stared at it. "It's for her," she said softly. "She's coming back."

Katya laid down the polishing cloth.

"No, lamb. No, your poor mother's not coming back tonight." She sighed.

Genia turned away, but curiosity wouldn't let her leave the room. When she turned back again, Aunt Katya was polishing a large-tined serving fork and her face had the pink tinge that always indicated she had major news or gossip to deliver. It was as though she was bursting with whatever it was she wanted to tell, and the pressure of her secret was straining against her skin, trying to be released. "We're having an important guest for dinner," she announced.

"Guest?"

"Indeed. A very distinguished person, coming to have supper with your poor father."

"My father?" she repeated stupidly. Most of the guests who'd come to the house were friends of her mother's. The rare visitors her father entertained were always official people, members of delegations from Czechoslovakia or Poland or, until last year's revolt, Hungary. They were never distinguished: drab engineers and dull bureaucrats. And no one at all had been to the house for the past two months. "Who is it?" Genia asked.

"Try to guess."

Genia shrugged. "It doesn't matter."

But Aunt Katya loved the game too much to let go. "Guess where he comes from."

"Africa?" It came out in spite of herself.

Katya laughed with delight. "Not Africa, my lamb, America!"

"Impossible."

"Not impossible. True. He comes directly from America." In her excitement, Aunt Katya had not forgotten to make Genia her tea. She now placed the glass in front of the girl.

"Capitalist or worker?"

"A rich capitalist, not a poor worker," Katya answered. They knew that America contained only two types of citizens. "You must wash your hair so it gleams."

Genia blew on the tea several times. It remained scorching. She left it on the kitchen table and ran to her father's study. He wasn't there, and she next tried the bedroom.

He was standing by the dresser, holding his boar-bristle hairbrush in one hand. In the other he held a small mirror and was inspecting himself in it. Genia had never seen him looking into a mirror before.

He smiled when she came in, a smile that would have been a grimace on a normal face, but she smiled back. He was wearing his braided military jacket, his hair was neatly brushed, and he stood erect. From the back, he could pass for an impressive man. "Genia, we are having a surprise."

"I know, the American. Aunt Katya told me—it's true?"

Giorgi nodded. "Put on your prettiest dress. Tonight you will meet a great friend to our country. Bernard Merritt."

"Who's he?"

"You have never heard the name of Bernard Merritt? No? He is an American and an industrialist, but nevertheless he is a friend of the Soviet Union."

Her father took on a new dimension of importance. The way he moved, held himself, and even his speech, more sonorous than usual. "Why is the American coming here?" Genia asked.

"To see me."

"Is he a friend of yours?" It was all mystifying, but in an exciting way.

Giorgi placed a stumpy finger to his lips. "We have business."

"Business . . . ?" Genia echoed, hoping for details, trying to understand more of what her father did.

"Of course, little one. To a capitalist, business always comes first."

"Before friendship?"

Giorgi sucked in his stomach and threw back his shoulders. Imitating a general, Genia thought, waiting for the reply.

"Get dressed now," he told her. "Aunt Katya will call you when it's time to come down."

She drew her own bath and lay in its soothing warmth for many minutes before she remembered her glass of tea. Too late now, but she didn't mind forgoing it, as she dipped her head back and her hair spread out over the water.

She soaped her hair, rinsed it and, with a sense of adventure ahead, washed all of her body meticulously, even between the toes. Coming out of the tub, she rubbed herself dry with quick movements of the towel, and took a second one to dry her hair. She used the remains of talc her mother had left behind, an exotic foreign powder in a flowered tin. As she applied it to herself—under her arms, between the legs, over her stomach—the subtle perfume reached her nostrils and Genia felt a moment's guilt. When she used to reach up from her bed for a good-night kiss, she would breathe in the wonderful scent of her mother, a scent that was mysterious and grown-up and beautiful but also a sad scent because after the kiss her mother would go away and then the perfume wafted slowly out of the room, erasing her traces.

On her own body, Genia could barely smell it after a minute or so. Maybe her mother used something else besides the talc, or maybe it was her mother's own smell, coming through the pores of her own skin, that was so wonderful. Other women didn't smell like that.

Did each woman have her own smell? When did she get it? Did it develop along with her body? If so, Genia thought, it would be a long time before she started smelling nice. Her own body looked more like a plank of wood than a woman. Her breasts were nearly as flat as Dmitri's; she didn't go in where women did, in the middle, and there was no fuzz between her legs. Vera Ivanova, Genia's best friend in the Pioneers, had fuzz *and* breasts. Mariusha Alexandreevna, who was much smaller than Genia, had been menstruating for more than a year. Genia didn't understand why she was being so slow about becoming a woman. Other girls did it easily, and none of their mothers were as beautiful as hers.

Now that her mother had gone, would she *ever* develop?

Even the pretty dress couldn't make her more womanly. It looked silly, she decided, as though she were costuming herself to look like somebody else. The dress had been her mother's once, and Aunt Katya had cut it down and reshaped it for her.

Despite Katya's compliments, Genia felt nervous as she walked down the stairs to meet the great man. She wished Dmitri were alongside her instead of already down there, as Katya had said.

When she entered the sitting room, a man with silver hair stood up, giving her a big smile. "You must be Genia. What a beautiful girl!"

He came over and took her hand. His eyes were sky blue, like glass marbles. His face was tanned, and the white collar of his shirt fitted so smoothly around his neck that it seemed molded. All the men's shirt collars she'd seen before were loose-fitting, usually open.

His suit was a soft blue-gray. She hadn't known suits could be anything but dark. The skin of his hands was soft, and his nails were perfectly shaped, clean, with a trim of white at the ends, pale moons at the bases.

"Wonderful dark eyes," he said.

She didn't know where to look. His pale eyes held her like a pinned butterfly. Looking into them was like looking up at the sky, trying to see through wispy clouds to the end of it. Once she'd tried that, lying on her back for hours until her eyes smarted and she felt dizzy. She was feeling dizzy now.

He was still looking at her as though memorizing each part of her face.

"This is Bernard Merritt," she heard her father's voice saying with importance. Genia shook her head up and down, biting her lip and blushing furiously.

He placed a hand gently at her elbow and led her back to where he'd been sitting. She would have preferred to become invisible. There was nothing she could possibly say to this person. She'd never seen anyone like him before.

"You must be a very clever girl," he said, "with eyes as intense as that."

She nodded, and blushed again.

"It's a proven fact," he began, his smile telling her that he was teasing, even though his words sounded serious, "that girls with hair like yours are destined to become leaders." His Russian was grammatically perfect, though his accent made it sound like a foreign language. "What's the word for the color of your hair?"

"Red."

It was Dmitri's answer. She hadn't noticed him until now.

The American shook his head. "It's auburn, chestnut. A rich, deep antique gold. In English, I'd call it 'titian.'"

Her lips silently repeated it. A beautiful word.

"Titian was a painter. His women have hair the color of yours, and pale skin like you have. He painted in the Renaissance, in Italy."

"In Russian, we call it 'red,'" Dmitri insisted. Genia felt his rudeness.

Their visitor ignored it. "Had I known that Secretary Sareyov had children, I would have brought you something too," he apologized to Genia, reaching into the inside pocket of his jacket. "Just a trinket, like this." He handed the thin box to Giorgi.

Inside lay a wristwatch with a gold band. "Waterproof," said Merritt.

Dmitri walked up to his father's chair and glanced down at the gift. "One of those. Tells time underwater. I've seen them before."

Genia drew in her breath tensely. She could feel Giorgi's anger about to strike. But he controlled it. "Magnificent," he said to Bernard Merritt. "You honor me." He went to the sideboard and brought back a heavy silver ashtray. "Please, accept this small souvenir of your visit to my house."

Genia was happy to see that the American looked at the ashtray attentively, turning it over in his hands. He didn't look at things, she decided; he studied them. He probably could understand everything, even inanimate objects.

Soon afterward, the men retired for dinner. They had business to discuss.

Dmitri shook hands with their guest, bowing slightly as he did, in an exaggeration of politeness. "Such an honor," he said. "*Mister* Merritt." He used the word *gaspodin*, "mister," instead of the usual *tovarich*, meaning "comrade."

"I hope we'll meet again, Dmitri. And you, too, Genia." Instead of shaking her hand, he raised it and lightly brushed his lips over her skin.

She was too flustered to say good night to her father, and only remembered when she was at the door. She turned, gave a little wave, and ran out.

In the kitchen, where Aunt Katya had set their places, she asked her brother angrily, "Why were you so rude?"

"Was I?" He raised an eyebrow.

"You know you were. It's shameful! You embarrassed everyone."

"Don't talk nonsense, Genia. Eat your dinner. You won't have lamb again for a long time."

She obeyed, chiefly because lamb was the most delicious of all meats, and they had it only on special occasions. But after two mouthfuls, she asked Dmitri again: "What were you doing, acting that way?"

"Don't put your nose in everything, Genuschka."

"Tell me!"

He put down his knife and fork and looked at her. Then he looked over at Aunty Katya. Genia understood that he would not speak freely in front of her. "Be patient, little sister. You'll soon learn more than you want to."

They finished the meal in silence. She remained angry at her brother. Bernard Merritt was the most fascinating man she'd ever met. Simply by looking at her, he had made Genia feel immeasurably valuable.

Bernard Merritt loved nothing more than possessions. Throughout the years, he'd acquired things—people, companies, and even countries, or at least franchises to their growth. What he couldn't own, he tried to control, sometimes of necessity from behind the scenes, pulling strings so nearly invisible that even his marionettes were unaware of them. He was astute, intuitive, ambitious, and sometimes sentimental.

Born into a family of less-than-modest means, Bernard started working at the age of eight, shining shoes with an older boy in the wealthy part of town. His angelic looks (blond curls, sky-blue eyes) earned him a small fortune in tips, and within five months he was operating on his own, his own shoebox monogrammed with his initials. At ten he'd expanded and was selling laces and shoe creams.

Throughout junior high and high school he worked, setting aside no time for homework. He didn't need it; his grades remained high and he received his diploma a few months short of sixteen.

His early years were a preview of the rest of his life. He was self-supporting by seventeen, married, divorced, and a millionaire by twenty-three, and launched in international trade at twenty-six. Three years later, in 1928, Bernard lost his millions. A temporary setback: he married an heiress the following year (and would acquire two more wives after that) and branched out in new forms of business. The Depression revived him and established him permanently as a major industrialist. Understanding that austerity meant that people could not afford necessities, Bernard concentrated on providing cheap luxuries. His companies made toys, Christmas ornaments, and, most profitably, cosmetics. His gamble worked; he'd predicted that women struggling with rent and food would put down a quarter for a new lipstick to make them "feel like a million bucks."

During the war he turned to machinery and raw materials, providing noninvolved nations (especially in Latin America) with plants, technicians, and know-how. Later he expanded to natural resources, to mining and drilling. By the late fifties, there remained few industries that Merritt had not at least tested.

Part of his love for possession and control was his pleasure in challenge. Bernard had been called "far-seeing," even "prophetic" in the press. What that meant was his ability to predict the needs or desires of his clients before they'd expressed them.

When he'd read the report of the Twentieth Congress of the Communist Party, in which Khrushchev revealed "crimes of the Stalin era" and denounced the "cult of personality" as evil, Bernard understood that the Soviet Union's foreign policy was about to change. The Congress had taken place in February 1956. Now, a little over a year later, there was not yet official sanction of East-West trade. But already Bernard's secret trips of the past year were beginning to show results. As Soviet policy was realigning itself, he was drawing up plans for the export of American farm materials and machinery. Khrushchev's priority was agriculture, and Bernard was waiting with a checklist of supplies. He'd arrived in Leningrad this morning, from Moscow.

"My meeting with the Chairman lasted thirty-five minutes," he reported over dinner. "I found him witty, keenly observant, and a fierce combatant. Khrushchev is a remarkable man."

Giorgi Sareyov nodded. He'd never met the Chairman, of course, but was flattered to have been chosen by him for the secret negotiations with Merritt. The seeming informality of the meeting—over dinner at home, introducing him to the children—was a perfect cover for their dealings. Merritt was in the country unofficially. In the United States, the Eisenhower government wasn't willing to discard the concept of a "Cold War" between the two major powers. Congress would never have approved the trip or its purpose. But both American and Soviet leaders were eager to open trade links with their old allies in the spirit of cooperation and peaceful coexistence.

"Chairman Khrushchev has basically approved my plan," said Bernard, taking a sip of the 1949 Château Haut-Brion. The Bordeaux indicated Sareyov's prestige. A lesser official would have served Georgian wine. "Though we have a number of details to iron out."

"Details, Comrade Merritt? You're referring to means of payment, I believe?"

Bernard smiled. "It will be years before the Soviet credit standing is reassigned. But I have one or two thoughts on how we might handle matters for the time being."

They spoke earnestly for the next two hours, returning to the sitting room after dinner for brandy and cigars. Each man knew the other's task. For Giorgi, unofficially representing the Soviet Ministry of Trade, it was to purchase the American equipment despite a short supply of dollars. Bernard, acting unofficially on behalf of the United States, offered a proposition for the Soviet payment which would increase their order—and at the same time enhance his prestige in America.

By the end of the evening, both were satisfied. Bernard offered to help the balance of trade by importing Russian dolls and other Soviet toys for both the North and South American markets. He also proposed a personal loan to the Soviet Union of twenty million dollars with extremely lenient terms for repayment.

He could afford to be generous. In addition to selling a larger amount of farm materials and machinery than he'd anticipated, Bernard had been promised by Giorgi that he personally would have "access to tokens in the history of religion." In other words, he would be able to smuggle priceless icons out of the country.

Giorgi was pleased with himself. Trading the past for the future. That was the way of a true Communist. He had once again vindicated the Party's trust in him.

Upstairs, in Dmitri's partition, Genia was sitting tailor-fashion on his bed in her woolen nightgown and socks. She was cold and would have liked to slip under the covers, but since that night when her brother had turned away from her, she'd vowed never to go into his bed again. Dmitri was sitting in his chair by the desk, still in the suit he'd put on to meet Bernard Merritt. The sleeves had become too short and the trouser cuffs had moved up to above his ankles since the last time he'd worn it, on his fifteenth birthday. Instead of making him look grown-up, the suit emphasized his boyishness. But he was beginning to sprout a mustache. Light from his desk lamp caught the thick, pale down above his upper lip. Genia watched it move as he read aloud to her from Khrushchev's special report to the Twentieth Congress: ". . . monstrous are the acts whose initiator was Stalin and which are rude violations of basic Leninist principles of—"

"It's boring," she protested.

He looked up with annoyance, his blue eyes tilted at the corners like their mother's. "Not boring at all, Genia. It's important that you understand. Our father is conferring at this moment with the American. Why is he in such a position?"

Genia held his eyes. She didn't know and didn't see why Dmitri bothered to ask. He'd been surly downstairs and now was being tedious. She wanted to go to her own bed and think about Bernard Merritt. He'd kissed her hand.

"I don't know either," he admitted, "but I've been reading and thinking a lot these past days. Father has held his position, whatever it is specifically, for many years. Eight of those were under Stalin. And now we know what Stalin was."

She waited, rubbing her toes to warm them.

"I'll try to make it simple, Genia. You believe in socialism, don't you?"

"Of course. Don't be stupid."

"And in the Party?"

"*Konechno*, of course."

Dmitri nodded. "*Konechno*. The party tells us Stalin was a criminal. He imprisoned and tortured innocent people, had them murdered. What was Father doing during that time?"

She didn't answer. Dmitri was only a schoolboy, she told herself. Even if he'd read a lot of books, he didn't know as much as he thought he did. "Father's always worked at home," she reminded him. "He isn't involved in all that."

"The second assumption doesn't follow," Dmitri said in an infuriatingly superior tone. "We don't really know anything about the work he does, except that he's with the Ministry of

Trade. What does that mean? It could be anything, even espionage."

"You're being crazy." She uncrossed her legs and swung them over the side of the bed.

"Don't go yet. Maybe it's not that. But what I want to know is how he maintains his position despite the change in leadership. I've gotten hold of some pamphlets, and I know that most of the people who had power under Stalin have disappeared. Dead, I guess. Think of Beria."

"Who's he?"

"Genia, you must learn to be more politically curious. Beria was in charge of the secret police, and was Stalin's presumed heir. He was at the deathbed of our 'Great Leader' four years ago. And then what happened to him? He was denounced as an international imperialist agent after Stalin died, and six months later was shot dead."

"Why are you telling me all this?"

"To make you see Father as he really is." He picked up the paper from his desk and read again: "'*Monstrous* are the acts . . .' A monster working for a monster."

"Don't say that!"

"Maybe she had good reason for leaving."

"She didn't! You're making all this up. I don't want to talk to you!" Genia was nearly at the door when Dmitri caught her. He took her in his arms and held her tightly against him. She felt him tremble. "I'm sorry, Genuschka, forgive me," he said softly. "I don't know why she left, but I must be able to forgive her."

"Why? Other mothers don't abandon their families. I never would."

He stroked her hair. "I love her."

"She deserted us!"

"I love her," he repeated, his voice choked. "And I'll find out why she had to leave. Because of *him*, I'm sure. What woman could live with a man like that? A freak?" Dmitri let her go.

Genia thought about his question. Her father's skin hung loose and waxen on his face. His nose was a hole, his fingers ugly roots. She shuddered at her own disloyalty.

"He was a hero," she offered lamely. "And before that he was handsome."

"I don't remember," said Dmitri. He'd been three when Genia was born. "I don't remember him at all from when I was very little. Only her. And Grandfather. The three of us lived together in the Hermitage, where they evacuated us after Grandfather's house was bombed. He died of starvation. He loved me a lot, Mother said."

Genia felt left out. Throughout her life, she'd often felt like an "extra" child with her mother, not a real one. Dmitri and Natasha somehow fit together. They were very similar. Each seemed to know what the other was thinking. Even when she was with both of them, she'd feel they were on an island by themselves.

Maybe, she'd thought, that was how things had to be. Mothers loved their sons most, and fathers their daughters. She was her father's favorite, Genia knew, but that didn't make her feel less deprived.

"Mother became an actress in Grandfather's theater when she was sixteen. That's only a year older than me now," he said wistfully. "I wonder what she looked like then."

"Like you, I suppose," Genia said unhappily. Her mother's hair must have been as light as his then, darkening over the years to a gleaming ocher. In comparison to her mother, Genia saw herself as plain. Her red hair was unattractive, her cheeks too plump. A few hours earlier, she'd felt beautiful, held in the pale iris of Bernard Merritt's gaze. But if her mother had been there, he wouldn't even have noticed Genia.

Aunt Katya knocked at the door and came in looking annoyed. She was usually asleep by this time, but she'd only now finished clearing and washing, setting out the plates for breakfast.

"What? You are still dressed in your clothes, Dmitri Giorgevitch? Do you know the time? Think of your poor sister. She'll be dead from tiredness in the morning." Taking Genia by the hand, Aunt Katya led her to bed.

She scolded her a little, and then relented, seating herself beside the bed. It had been an exciting evening and she could see the child was still wrought up, her eyes bright, not even sleepy. She decided to stay a few minutes, in case Genia wanted to confide in her, and drew out her sewing from the deep pocket in her apron. She hated letting time go to waste.

Genia watched the needle coming up rhythmically from the material, pulling the thread taut. "What're you sewing?" she asked.

Aunt Katya held it up and Genia recognized the old doll with its cloth face. Scha-scha, she'd named it when she was very little. She'd forgotten it over the years.

"I found it in a box with your mother's things," Aunt Katya said. "I remembered how you loved playing with it." The linen of the face was torn and stained, a small flap of cloth hung down from the cheek. "See how badly you treated the poor little thing."

Genia reached out and took it from her hands. She studied the face a moment, the neat seam where Katya had begun repairing it. She spoke her thoughts aloud. "Why can't someone mend people like this? People with torn faces?"

Aunt Katya sighed. "Little angel, we must trust in Our Savior."

"I was hoping for something a little more practical," Genia said curtly as she handed back the doll.

Giorgi Sareyov poured another glass of brandy for each of them. Holding out his glass, he said, "To our agreement! To Soviet-American friendship!"

"To peace!" Bernard Merritt added, raising his glass to the same level as his host's.

They drank. "And now you must call me Giorgi Mikhailovitch."

"And you call me Bernard." They clinked glasses and drank again. "I'm very glad to have met you tonight," Bernard said. "I've been curious about you for some time."

"Why?"

"Your name came up often concerning trade decisions." Bernard smiled. "Yet none of the people who talked about you had ever met you. And it seemed a little . . . well, odd, that you weren't in Moscow."

Giorgi held his glass against his cheek. "Now you know," he said abruptly. "I am not fit to be seen."

"I've heard of your heroism during the siege."

"Have you?" Giorgi's voice was not pleasant.

"You were brutally tortured by the Nazis," Bernard said quietly.

"Yes. They needed no weapons. They made good use of the ice. They kept my face in it until the skin froze to it, ice and flesh joined together as solid as stone—then they ripped it off."

Bernard studied the amber liquid in his glass. "Do you know Semyon Grollinin?"

"In the Politburo? Yes."

"I heard he was also disfigured during the siege."

"He was."

"He underwent plastic surgery."

"So they say."

"A series of operations. In the West."

Giorgi spoke very slowly at first, drawing each word out like yarn from a tangled ball. "I was on the ice for many months bringing supplies. I knew how to take care of myself. When they captured me, I was still strong. I resisted them. I didn't tell those putrid fascists a thing." He thrust his hands in front of Bernard. "Look! I was a machinist before the war. They destroyed my fingers one by one. I didn't cry out. Not ever. I didn't beg. I didn't let them see how deeply I felt the pain. I knew that what they were doing to my country was far worse. They were murdering my city. They were starving her, torturing Leningrad, brutalizing her. More than a million of us died, Bernard." His voice broke.

Bernard watched his face as he listened attentively. Giorgi took a deep breath and began again. "The dead were the more fortunate. The survivors had to endure the unendurable. Our children died painfully before our eyes. Our water was contaminated and stank from rotting corpses. We became cannibals; we ate our own dead. *They* did it to us. The Nazis turned us into beasts."

He was silent for so long, staring at a spot on the carpet, that Bernard finally said: "It would seem that you'd want to forget all that, and bury the past."

"Never!" Giorgi looked up sharply, his eyes focused on Bernard's. "Don't you see? I'm a part of it, I belong to it. They made me into this . . . what I am today. It was they in the end who took my wife from me. They, the self-proclaimed master race. Not one of them fit to be called human. They stripped me of everything but my hatred—and I wear it on my face."

After a few minutes Bernard got up. Giorgi went with him to the door. In silence they shook hands, Bernard taking Giorgi's in both his own, affirming a new tie between them.

3

Cross-legged on the woven rug from Tashkent, Genia
paused in her crocheting to look into the fire, its flickering
tongues outlined in deep orange, filled in with yellow. It was
restless and animated, the opposite of the ice that still locked
the Neva, holding the river in a deathly grip.

Fire and ice were opposites, like life and death, mother and
father. Her mother sparkled. Her fingers, racing over piano
keys or dancing to accompany her words, were never still. Her
cheeks were rosy, like Genia's. She wore bright colors and
strings of beads that caught the light, refracting it into tiny
rainbows against her smooth skin.

Footsteps were coming closer to the sitting room, and Genia
quickly put her handiwork underneath her. She was crocheting a cap for Aunt Katya in bright green wool, and even though
today was Sunday, when Katya usually slipped away to church
(she didn't think anyone knew where she was going), Genia
didn't want to take a chance of spoiling the surprise.

But the footsteps were heavy, uneven. Genia turned from
the fire to look up at her father as he entered the room. She
shuddered with an old memory. Waking up at night—it was
before the partition, when Dmitri's bed stood next to hers, but
he wasn't in it—she was crying out from a bad dream. Her
covers had fallen off the bed and she thought she was freezing
to death. As she cried, the door had opened. Her father was

leaning over her. Pale light from the hallway made his face a dull gray blob as she looked up at him and screamed. He straightened and walked out, without retrieving her blankets from the floor.

"What are you sitting on, my beauty?" He squatted beside her on his haunches.

She brought it out. "For Aunty Katya."

He hardly glanced at the small circle of wool, spiraling out from the ring at the center. "I must tell you something."

She drew back, afraid of his tone.

"Your mother has been arrested."

She turned to the fire, its crowded tongues reaching for air. "The actor too?"

"No. Not him. The reports say she was taken away last night. She alone. Separated from her lover."

"What has she done? Why was she arrested?" Genia had been thinking of Natasha as vanished, away from Leningrad, not even in Russia. Strange now to feel she was somewhere near.

"She's under suspicion, that's all I know." Something in her father's voice made Genia look at him. A note of satisfaction? "There'll be a hearing sometime in the next weeks. I'll do what I can to help her, for the sake of the past."

She didn't believe he would help her mother. Was she guilty of an awful crime and had she run away to escape justice with no time even to leave a note?

"When the hearing takes place, I might ask you and Dmitri to come with me. You're nearly thirteen and the court may listen to you."

"What can I say? I don't know anything."

"She's your mother. You can tell the court what kind of a mother she was to you. About her character and so forth."

"When?"

"When the time comes." He stood and looked down at his daughter, her hair in the firelight gleaming with high polish. He placed his hand on her head and felt her stiffen. "I'll see you at suppertime," he said in sorrow.

She stared into the flame, hoping Dmitri would be back soon to help her wrestle with the news. Ever since he'd made her aware of their father's position and the secrecy surrounding it, she'd become wary. Such an important man could surely find out more about the reasons for his wife's arrest.

She hated having to doubt him, and was angry at her

brother for planting suspicion. He'd always been antagonistic toward their father, particularly since their bitter fight last summer when Dmitri turned fifteen and refused to join the Komsomol. Giorgi ordered him to, saying he was a child and had no right to a decision. But Dmitri stood firm, insisting that if he were forced to join he'd attend no meetings. "To be a good Communist doesn't mean you have to run with a pack of sheep," she remembered him saying. At the time it sounded important and philosophical.

Their mother had defended him, arguing that a boy of fifteen was a young man and entitled to his opinions. If they were mistaken, he would find out soon enough to correct them.

But Giorgi didn't listen. A light froth of spittle had gathered at the corner of his mouth as he accused his son of being a "traitor" and slapped him across the face.

Dmitri had turned white, and though later that day Giorgi had begged his pardon, Genia knew that her brother never had, and never would, forgive him.

Her father was quick to anger, a prey to moods. He was often extreme, but she'd always trusted him. But why did she feel now that he knew more than he was telling her? That he was hiding something?

She picked up the crocheting, but dropped stitches all around the circle. At the end of the row, she pulled it out and began to do it over. Again she lost count, made errors, and dragged out the wool. She repeated the circular row a third time, bungled again, and in a fit of frustration pulled out all the stitches, leaving a wobbly line of wool clustered on itself like thin green entrails.

She placed the guard in front of the fire and went for her coat. She'd go visit Vera. They'd look through her scrapbooks at the pressed flowers, old photographs, the little drawings of birds and horses. Vera was an avid collector of what she called "the true and the beautiful." This could mean flowers, feathers, or even stones in a peculiar shape. The rusted piece of a car bumper was Vera's most prized possession. In its corrosion she saw intricate patterns and an array of colors. Vera wanted to be a cosmonaut when she grew up, mainly so she could look down at the earth and see all of it at once, a bright blue ball, as she imagined, suspended in space.

Vera's father, Ivan Malchikoff, was the foreman of a factory. Her mother, Elena, was a construction engineer. They were friendly, easygoing people who always gave Genia a warm welcome, particularly since her mother had left.

Genia hadn't invited Vera home after her first visit, when they'd passed her father in the hall and Vera had stared as though she couldn't decide what manner of thing he was. Since then, the girls always met at Vera's apartment.

Genia was halfway there when she remembered she'd not told anyone where she was going. Aunt Katya would be back from church and would be looking for her. Her father would worry. She walked more slowly, deliberating whether or not to turn back, when she noticed a commotion farther down the street, people rushing up to join a circle forming around what looked to be a horse-drawn cart. She hurried toward it.

As she came closer, she could see the white breathing of both horses. The driver of the cart was gesticulating and shouting. People were leaning forward, looking at something on the ground at the center. She made her way to the front of the crowd.

He was lying in the street, eyes closed, the right sleeve of his dark gray jacket ripped into tatters. Genia screamed.

Dmitri opened his eyes as she knelt beside him. His skin was grayish, his features accordioned in pain.

"Leg," he gasped. She looked down at the blood seeping from below his right trouser leg, a thick red soup dripping onto the cobblestones.

Two women were running toward them. One of them knelt on the other side of Dmitri and began cutting the trouser leg with a knife. She seemed to be a doctor, and was telling the crowd to move back. She paid no attention to Genia as she pulled the material away and felt along Dmitri's leg, along the thigh, down the calf. When she reached his ankle, Dmitri howled.

The doctor frowned. "It's not his leg," she muttered to herself, and tried to take off his shoe.

But Dmitri gave a shrill cry when she touched the shoe. He was breathing heavily, his lips moving as though he were trying to explain. All that came out was "no" and "please."

The doctor got off her knees and told the other woman, "His foot's been crushed. We need a stretcher." Genia saw that his right shoe was badly battered and at a strange angle to the rest of his leg.

She pulled off her jacket, made it into a pillow, and gently raised Dmitri's head onto it. He tried to smile. "No," he mumbled. "Cold."

"Never mind." She didn't feel the cold, only her helplessness.

Someone brought a flask to his lips, and he sipped the vodka. Then the men arrived with a stretcher and carefully moved Dmitri onto it. He kept his teeth clenched to make no sound, but perspiration bathed his face.

One of the men handed Genia her jacket. She put it on and followed them for about a kilometer's walk to the hospital. She kept her eyes on her brother every moment, seeing each jolt of the stretcher register on his face, feeling the pain in her own body.

At the hospital, she learned that Dmitri had been walking home from a soccer game, passing the cart just as a large bird suddenly swooped in front of the horses, causing them to rear. He'd tried to grab the reins of the horse closest to him, but was thrown to the ground, the rein caught around his wrist. As the horses cantered on, he was dragged along and the wheels of the cart ran over his foot, mangling it.

His big toe had been severed, and many small bones were splintered, a nurse told Genia. They would operate immediately, but there was no hope of restoring the foot to normal. Dmitri would be left with a severe limp.

A few days later, Dmitri was still in the hospital when Bernard Merritt came again for dinner. Aunt Katya surpassed herself with the meal. In honor of their special guest she'd made delicious little *piroschki* to serve with the soup, meat pastries smaller than a mouthful. Usually Genia ate a dozen or more at a time, but tonight she had no appetite, even for them. She toyed with the soup, too, taking only a few spoonfuls of *schchi*, the steaming cabbage soup prepared according to a recipe from her grandmother. She felt ill-at-ease, seated between her father in his bulky jacket and Bernard, whose perfectly tailored suit was just a shade darker than his skin.

Bernard Merritt looked at her in that strange way again, fixedly, taking her up in his sky-blue eyes. Genia was sure he could see right through her, into her thoughts and through to her very soul. She cast her eyes down to the tablecloth.

Though Genia didn't believe in a God, she knew that

everyone had a soul, even animals. Dmitri's soul was like a young green twig, flexible and growing. Her father had a soul like the river Neva, a turbulent depth hidden by the surface. Bernard Merritt? She looked over at him from the corner of her eye and tried to imagine what his soul was like. All she could picture were his eyes, pale blue and clouded like a marble. Maybe American souls were different from Russian.

Noticing the child's shyness, he tried to draw her out by asking about Dmitri's accident. Her shyness was in itself a small challenge and Bernard felt compelled to meet it.

Within minutes she was talking freely and with animation. When the main dish was brought in—cutlets Pojarski in a rich mushroom sauce—she attacked the food with an enthusiasm that made Bernard smile broadly. He wasn't used to children, but he enjoyed their uninhibited behavior, their surrender to impulse.

He observed that Genia's childhood was in its last stage of chrysalis, soon to be discarded as she emerged into young womanhood. Sareyov's little girl would grow up to be a stunner, he predicted, and wondered for a moment if he'd ever see her as a woman. The reshuffling in party leadership could end Sareyov's influence, potentially his career. Bernard was aware of enough changes of direction over the past thirty-five years to know that no Soviet official's position was secure.

"They told you there was *no chance* of restoring the foot to normal?" Bernard repeated.

Genia nodded.

He turned to her father. "Are you accepting this prognosis?"

Giorgi shrugged. "The doctors do what they can. It was a bad accident, multiple breaks. Bones splintered, tore through nerves and muscles. And the toe—it's not taking."

"But we must talk to the doctors. We must see what can be done, now or in the future."

Giorgi looked down at his plate, frowning. Genia kept staring at Bernard, feeling he would make everything right. He would make Dmitri walk normally again, just by the force of his will.

The expression of adoration on the girl's face goaded Bernard. "Giorgi Mikhailovitch, we must explore all possibilities. The boy is only fifteen, still growing. We must make sure he gets every chance. I'll make an appointment—"

"I can do that myself," said Giorgi coldly.

"Do!" Genia begged.

"There's no need," her father reminded her. "Our doctors are always available during their office hours."

"We'll go then," Bernard said. "Tomorrow. Settled." Giorgi looked at him, opened his mouth, and then brought his lips back together in a tight line as he angrily waved off Katya, who was bringing around a second helping.

Bernard, too, refused more cutlets. When Katya was clearing off the dishes, replacing them with dessert plates, Bernard excused himself a moment and came back with a package for Genia, wrapped in shiny purple-and-white-striped paper.

It was almost too beautiful to open. Genia carefully removed the purple ribbon and put it aside to wear in her hair. She unwrapped the gleaming paper and found four flat purple-and-white-striped boxes inside. Each of these held three identical pairs of nylon stockings, a pale honey shade in the first box, becoming a tone darker in each succeeding box. Bernard reached for one of the stockings and slipped it over his fist to demonstrate how it looked against the skin.

Genia did the same, noticing how different the sheer color appeared against her own hand. The nylon dusted her skin, making it smooth and tanned. She blushed. Such finery was meant for a grown woman.

"You like them?"

"Beautiful." Impulsively she kissed Bernard on the cheek, not noticing that her father winced at the spontaneous affection she could show to a stranger, but not to him.

Next afternoon, as usual, Genia went directly from school to the hospital. She held her breath walking through the men's ward to her brother's bed, feeling that the eyes of the sick and injured men were reproaching her for being healthy, young, and a girl. Someone called out, "Hey! Hello, little flower. Come over and let me sniff you!" But Genia hurried toward Dmitri.

He was sitting up, pale as the sheets, his mouth set as a grim scar in his face. The daisies she'd brought him two days before were dying already, petals missing like the teeth of an old man. The water had evaporated in the bottle that held them.

She kissed him. "I wish they'd let you come home. I want to take care of you."

"Genuschka," he greeted her dully, edging to the side of the bed to make room. She was afraid of adding to his pain by sitting there. He was too brave to complain, but sometimes the pain passed over his face and he looked frightened. "Sit," he insisted, patting the sheet.

She perched gingerly. "Any more news of the arrest?" he asked.

"No."

"The hearing—has it been set?"

"No. At least, I haven't heard."

"Bastard," he muttered softly. "I'm sure he's behind it."

"You're imagining things. You want to pretend she's perfect and innocent. But the truth may be that she ran away because of her crimes—she was afraid Father would find out."

"Don't be a stupid child!" he shouted, leaning forward. Pain yanked him back to the pillow. "How can you forget? *You're* the one who's pretending. You're so eager to side with *him* that you've lost your memory. Think about her. Picture her. How could such a woman commit a crime?"

"She ran away. She ran away with another man, and she didn't even leave a note."

"I don't believe that either."

"You don't believe anything that's under your nose."

"On the contrary, sister dear," he said in his terrible cold voice, "it's you who won't see anything. I'm sure she left a note—she was always leaving messages for us when she went out. It's not in her character to leave without a word."

"Where is it, then?"

"Ask *him.*"

"Are you saying he destroyed the note?"

"Yes, and I'm also saying he's the one who had her arrested."

"Your broken foot has made you lose your mind. He's going to *defend* her. He told me he'd help her for the sake of the past. He asked me to come along, and you too, so we could *help* her." Genia was nearly crying, her voice becoming more and more insistent as she tried to drown out her own doubts.

When Dmitri didn't answer, just turned his blond head to the side, she began to plead. "He wouldn't do anything like that, would he? Why would he want to destroy the note? Tell me that."

Dmitri, who had lost his virginity eight months earlier, on the day after his violent quarrel with his father, answered, "Sexual jealousy."

Genia tried to reason: "It makes no sense. A person doesn't

have someone arrested so he can defend her. A person doesn't destroy a note left for someone else."

He gave her a hard stare. "Can't you understand? Natalya Leonova was—is—a beautiful woman. A talented actress. A woman filled with love. Everything that *he* isn't, that he could never reach. He has a deformed soul, like his face. Nothing but hatred grows there."

Genia was shocked by his vehemence. "He loves us," she protested.

"You, maybe. Me, he hates. He's afraid of me—"

"You're making up—"

"Yes, he is! He knows that I can see through him, to the black hole he carries as a heart."

Speaking like that, Dmitri reminded Genia of their father, full of passion.

She noticed the two men coming up the ward before Dmitri did: the silver-haired foreigner in his impeccable suit, the disfigured man thumping alongside. She felt the stares accompanying them.

When they were nearly at the foot of his bed, Dmitri saw them and shrank back. Then he pulled himself erect, his lips in a sardonic expression. "Mr. Merritt. An honor. Forgive me for not getting to my feet."

Genia rose and went over to the men. Bernard smiled at her and asked Dmitri, "How are you feeling?"

"Ever so well, thank you. And you?"

"There's no point," said Giorgi. "He's playing the martyr."

Bernard looked from father to son, sensing the battle between them. He'd left his own father, and his home, when he'd been about as old as Dmitri. A boy that age could take care of himself. But the foot was rotten luck.

"What do the doctors predict?" Bernard asked Dmitri.

"That when I walk again, I shall do it badly."

"Did they mention the possibility of reconstructive surgery, later on perhaps?"

Dmitri looked exhausted on the pillows. Genia felt torn. She wanted Bernard to help, and she could see her brother wanted to be left alone.

"No," he answered wearily. "They didn't. We are not in the West, Mr. Merritt."

"Makes no difference," said Giorgi angrily. "The West is not more advanced. You see"—he turned to Bernard—"our doctors and surgeons have had the distinct advantage of war. They

trained on the battlefield, they did their research under fire.
We are a technological country, Bernard, a scientific one, and
our medical advances are second to none."

Dmitri looked at his father, opened his mouth as though to
speak, and closed it again. A faint smile played on his lips.

The ward doctor approached the bed, raising her eyebrows
at the visitors, an indication that they should leave.

"Comrade doctor . . ." Bernard began.

"Yes?" The blond woman looked at him coldly, reading in his
foreign clothes and strange accent an unmistakable affront to
her authority.

"When you're finished, I'd like to speak to you. About this
young man . . ."

"You are the father?"

"No."

"If the boy's father wishes to speak to me, I shall be available
later on. Now, if you will let me examine the patient." She took
hold of his wrist, facing him, her back to the two men.

Genia walked with them down the ward, embarrassed by
the doctor's rudeness. Giorgi, too, host in his own country, was
uncomfortable. "She's following rules," he apologized. "Members of a hospital staff are not empowered to speak to
outsiders."

Bernard accepted the apology. She was an underling; he'd
deal with superiors. "I understand. You'll go talk to her?"

"Yes," Giorgi promised. A few minutes later he and Genia
went into the shared offices to wait.

Bernard returned to Dmitri's bedside. He wanted to speak
to the boy alone. He needed to learn everything he could
about Giorgi Sareyov.

Though Giorgi had reported to him that the basic outline for
the farm deal had been accepted by Soviet authorities, many
obstacles still remained before actual trading could begin.
Bernard was still not certain whether Giorgi was just a puppet
following orders from above, or was a policymaker, moving
slowly to protect himself from internal criticism.

Bernard had noticed, and taken into account, Dmitri's
antagonism toward his father. The son might reveal aspects of
Giorgi that could help Bernard in his negotiations. He might,
for instance, make clear the matter of his mother, Giorgi's wife.
She was a Jew, Bernard had learned, who'd been arrested and
was about to be tried on unspecified charges. Was there a
revival of anti-Semitism in the Soviet Union? And what

implications would that have on Giorgi Mikhailovitch's future, and on the validity of his transactions?

Looking at Dmitri, the fair boy with blue eyes, it was impossible to tell that he was half Jewish. Without preamble, Bernard asked him: "About your mother—do you have an opinion?"

Dmitri shrugged.

"Could the arrest have been a mistake?" Standing beside Dmitri's bed because there were no chairs, Bernard knew he appeared like an inquisitor, questioning from above.

"It could be," said Dmitri carefully.

"Would it help your mother if the hearing were publicized? If news of it were leaked to the foreign press?"

"What we do in this country is our own affair, Mr. Merritt. If we make mistakes, we can always remedy them." He was echoing his mother's words at the time of his argument with Giorgi. He had no reason to trust an American.

Bernard abandoned the line of questioning for the moment. "When will you be able to leave the hospital?" he asked noncommittally.

"I'm not sure. A week, maybe two."

"And then?"

"Crutches for four months. When I throw off my crutches"—he gave a harsh chuckle—"I shall be lame."

"I might be able to help. Through my dealings with your country over the years, I've made a number of friends who would be willing to do me a favor—"

"Mr. Merritt," Dmitri interrupted, "I am a Soviet citizen. I don't need special privileges. You see me here on the ward with other men. Some are laborers, some students like myself. Others are managers. In your country, you would have a private room, a private nurse, and a private doctor. You would have special meals prepared for you, and bring all the specialists to your assistance." He winced as a wave of pain broke over his face. "Privilege means power. Capitalism is dedicated to the cause of self-interest. Thank you for your offer, Mr. Merritt, but it's not for me."

Bernard felt a flash of anger. But he held out his hand and Dmitri took it, looking up at Bernard with a proud expression. So like his father, Bernard thought.

* * *

Dmitri was still in the hospital on the day of the hearing in mid-April.

Genia wore her Pioneer outfit, as her father had asked her to, with high white socks. She'd thought of the nylon stockings, but felt right away that they'd be somehow suspect. Aunty Katya braided her hair for her, as though she were a little girl, crying as she folded the thick plaits into each other.

Giorgi wore his military uniform. When they entered the courtroom, a voice called out, "Secretary Giorgi Mikhailovitch Sareyov!" Genia saw the judge remove her steel-rimmed spectacles and look across at them, her face wearing the same startled expression that came to most people at the sight of Genia's father.

Genia sat erect on the bench, her father next to her, rigid, with hands clenched. She could smell his perspiration, a thin sourness that made her feel queasy. She was cold, despite her sweater. The room was gray and so large it seemed empty, even with the people in it; like a mausoleum.

She leaned forward to get away from the smell. The procurator was standing near the judge, proclaiming and gesticulating, but she couldn't understand him. The strange words, technical terms, poured out from him, all gibberish to Genia, and his arms swept the air in large arcs to indicate the enormity of his accusations.

She couldn't picture it, and even though her father had told her, Genia couldn't really believe that her mother would make an appearance here. Such drama didn't suit her. At home, she used to recite long passages from Chekhov or Gorky to a small audience of friends, and she'd make everyone smile or chuckle despite the sadness of the plays.

"Bring out the accused, Natalya Leonova Sareyov!"

A guard escorted her in, then released her and she moved toward the stand alone, walking with slow, small steps as though her feet were chained.

Genia saw her mother grab hold of the railing around the stand to steady herself. She blinked rapidly, drew herself up, and looked out into the room.

Genia's heart pounded against her ears, drumming out all other sounds. She stared at her mother. Blue eyes fringed with dark lashes, skin pale as snow. She looked incredibly fragile, and beautiful.

"This woman is part of a conspiracy aimed at the destruction of our socialist state . . ."

Genia couldn't take her eyes away, but her vision blurred, looking at the face she'd known all her life. Over the past months she'd tried to erase it from her mind. But now her mother was standing in front of her, raised on a small platform, her face unbearably intimate. Genia wanted to run up and beg her mother to come home. She felt her father's hand on her hip, restraining her, making her feel hot and ashamed. She wanted never to see her mother again as long as she lived.

She was hypnotized by the figure on the stand as it moved in and out of focus. The voice of the man droned and peaked.

"We have countless testimonies and signed statements against you. They accuse you of deviationism and moral turpitude. Of cosmopolitanism.

"You are a traitor, Natalya Leonova, worse than a thief, more devious than a murderer.

"A thief takes what belongs to others, but only their possessions. You have stolen the trust of the people by violating the principles of Marxism-Leninism. You have stolen the trust of your own family, and of the Soviet Socialist People's Republic. You have murdered our hope in the future."

The procurator finished speaking. The judge asked if anyone in the courtroom had something to say. No one answered. She called on Comrade Sareyov: "Is there any information you might have, as the accused's husband, to influence the court's decision?"

Giorgi Mikhailovitch stood up slowly, not looking in his wife's direction. "Comrade judge, I would do anything to help her," he said. "For the sake of the children. This little girl here"—he swept his arm toward Genia—"is our daughter. She needs a mother. But her mother left her, and her brother, to join a circle of drifters.

"I believe the children have not yet been corrupted. In their interest, and in loyalty to our party and our country, I must defer to the judgment of this court. If the accused is found guilty, she must be removed from society to prevent contagion. If she is declared to be innocent, I welcome her, as a loving husband and patriotic citizen, back into our home and our socialist society."

A light sprinkle of applause greeted his words. Giorgi sat down again, perspiring heavily.

"You are very young, Evgenia Giorgovna, but I have before me a special commendation of you by the Pioneers. In recognition of your mature attitude, the court permits you to speak on behalf of your mother, if you choose." The judge looked at her through thick circles of glass.

Genia opened her mouth.

"Stand up, please, when you address the court."

Genia looked at her mother, held her eyes. She got to her feet. Her lips moved, but no sound came. She flung her arms open. "Why . . . ?" she began in a high, child's voice.

"Why what?" the judge prompted. "Speak up."

Her arms out in front of her, eyes locked with her mother's, Genia asked, "Why didn't you leave me a note?"

She was beginning to sob as her father pulled her back to her seat.

4

On the first of May, every city of the USSR celebrates the most important holiday of the year with parades and demonstrations to reaffirm the solidarity of workers.

On this May Day, Genia wasn't marching with her Pioneer group. Dmitri had been released from the hospital the day before, and she stayed home to keep him company.

"An unnecessary sacrifice," he said with disapproval. He was still weak, mainly from inactivity.

"It's not a sacrifice," Genia insisted. For the past two weeks, since the day of the hearing, she'd lost her enthusiasm for everything, even the Pioneers. She felt a persistent sense of nausea and couldn't eat. Alarmed, Aunt Katya prepared new delicacies every day, but Genia could barely tolerate even their smell. "Your soul is troubled," Katya diagnosed.

After her mother had been led away, Genia had followed her father out of the courthouse into the waiting limousine, a streamlined black Zil. Inside, her father had placed his arm around her shoulder and she'd remained completely still, a prisoner of his touch and of the odor emanating from him, rancid in the enclosed air.

"All is for the best, *krasavitzsa maya*, my beauty," he'd said to her profile. "I'll make a good life for you, you'll see." His heavy hand patting her shoulder up and down, up and down, had felt like an anvil pounding her into the seat. Then his hand had stopped pumping and hung limply from the edge of Genia's shoulder. They hadn't spoken again all the way home.

And not after they'd reached the house either. She'd seen Giorgi carry a bottle of vodka from the kitchen upstairs to his bedroom, and the nausea had been with her then and had kept coming back since that day.

"You're more important than a parade," Genia said, tucking the blankets around Dmitri in his armchair. "I prefer being with you."

"Not just a parade, Genia. It's a demonstration of unity. Workers uniting under the banner of *mir y drujhba*, peace and friendship." There were downstairs in the sitting room, Dmitri's injured foot resting on a hassock in front of the fireplace. "Has *he* gone out?"

"Yes."

"To frighten the masses."

Genia shrugged. She knew it was complicated for her father, being seen in public. Normally he avoided contact with anyone but those entering his household. Yet, as an important official he had a duty to join the May Day proceedings. "He tries to hide."

"He should bury himself!" Dmitri said cruelly. "No one should ever have to see that hideous mug of his again."

"I think he feels a little of that himself," Genia said, barely understanding what she was trying to convey. She knew he'd been quite drunk when he left the house earlier in the morning, and she'd recognized the mood he'd been in, though "mood" wasn't the right word. She sensed that it was a kind of double-being, his two selves pulling him apart, though she couldn't put the thought into words, even to herself.

"He's too ugly to be invited on the reviewing stand," Dmitri went on, "so he has to go among the ordinary people. It's not fair to them."

And to him? Genia wondered, but she said nothing, sitting on the floor next to her brother's chair.

"Breakfast!" Aunt Katya trilled, coming in with a large tray. On it were bowls of farmer's cheese and sour milk. Genia shook her head.

"You must eat," Katya implored. "You always loved this. You ate bowls and bowls of it." She turned to Dmitri for support. "Tell her, please. She's wasting away. Touches nothing. Like a little bird our Genia is now!"

"She'll eat when she's hungry." Dmitri automatically defended his sister. But when Katya had left the room he asked with concern, "You're not eating? How long has this been going on?"

"It's my stomach. I have cramps . . ."

Dmitri looked down at her, furrow between his eyebrows. Then he smiled. "You're getting to be a big girl, Genuschka. That's what it is. In nine days you'll be thirteen. It's time. You're becoming a woman." His smile broadened and he opened his arms.

She jumped up and kissed him, then pulled back, laughing. "It's not that, you silly!"

"No? What then?"

She went back down to the floor and resumed her tailor position, looking into the bare fireplace. "It's . . . the hearing."

"Of Mother?"

Genia nodded mutely.

"Of course you're upset. You shouldn't have gone. He had no business dragging you there. Made no difference to the outcome—that was determined before the trial began."

She wished she could believe that. "I don't think so," she answered slowly. "I behaved like a fool. A baby. I could have said something . . ."

"No." Dmitri placed his hand comfortingly on her head. "Don't think that, Genuschka. A political trial is a matter of state policy. It doesn't concern itself with individuals."

She wanted to tell him everything. Maybe then the nausea would leave her. "Father didn't . . . defend her."

"How could he?"

She looked up in amazement. Dmitri handed her his empty bowl and spoon, and she placed them on the floor. Then she looked up at him again.

"Giorgi Mikhailovitch belongs to the Party and represents its concerns. He's not a private man. At a political hearing he appears in his official position and speaks *for* it and *through* it. The Party represents social order."

"But you loved her!" Genia cried.

"I do! But our mother was always politically naive, like you. She lived for art and beauty and ignored the realities of politics. It's possible that she *was* misled by others."

"You think she was guilty?" Genia asked incredulously.

"No. Not guilty of any crime except the failure to mistrust people."

"Then why was she convicted?"

"Because"—Dmitri's voice sounded very tired—"her actions may have been misinterpreted, perhaps intentionally to suit the Party's purpose."

"Then the Party's wrong!"

He gave a faint smile. "You're just like her. Maybe it was a mistake. Mistakes will be made again and again until we reach our goal of a just and peaceful society. At the trial, did the word 'Jew' come up?"

"No, I don't think so."

"'Zionist'? 'Zionism'?"

"No. I didn't hear it."

"'Cosmopolitanism'?"

"Maybe. It was so confusing . . ."

"Help me up, will you?" he asked wearily. "It's the same thing. In the Doctor's Plot against Stalin the Jewish doctors were accused of cosmopolitanism. You have to learn to read between the lines, Genuschka, and to hear the words that are only thought, not spoken."

She brought him his crutches and walked behind him as Dmitri hobbled up the stairs. She helped him into bed, arranged his pillows, and kissed him on the forehead. "You're my brother, and sometimes I feel I don't know you."

"You do, Genuschka." He smiled wanly. "As well as anyone. I'm an optimist and a cynic. Socialism is an optimistic belief. Capitalism isn't. Communism is a goal, an ideal, and I often doubt that we'll ever achieve it unless we give up some of our rigidity and blindness. Or go to sleep."

He closed his eyes and Genia stood looking at him for a few minutes, until she saw that his breathing was deep and regular. Then she realized she was hungry and ran down to the kitchen.

On the morning of her birthday, Genia found her father at the breakfast table, wearing a freshly ironed shirt, his hair carefully combed. He stood up when she entered, and seemed nervous. "Could I give you a kiss?" he asked. "This is an important day."

She couldn't refuse, and after she'd held out her cheek to him, Giorgi reached under his chair and brought up a package wrapped in newspaper. "For you," he said shyly.

He watched as she opened it, fearing even at the last minute that he'd chosen badly, that it would be too large or too small, maybe not to her taste. It was the first present he'd bought for her on his own since Genia was born. Natasha had made all the purchases.

For this, Genia's thirteenth birthday present, Giorgi had gone to the foreign store, braving the stares, the embarrassed jerk of a head when he caught someone looking at him. It had been a nightmare, but he'd done it for Genia.

"It's nice," she said. "Thank you."

He remembered how she'd run up to Bernard and kissed his cheek.

"Is it," he begged, "the right color?"

"It's very pretty." The blouse was a dark rose, a beautiful color, but Genia with her red hair had stayed away from pinks and reds. "I'll wear it tonight," she promised, and her father smiled.

He'd offered to give a party for her, and Genia had refused at first, because there was no one she dared ask to her house. But Giorgi had implored her to have it, and in the end she'd invited Vera, adding, as if casually, that her father would be home; and Mariusha Alexandreevna, whose parents were friends of Giorgi's.

"I have something else for you." He reached down under his chair again and brought up a strange-looking object made of black metal.

"It's from a machine, from the factory where I used to work before the war. My fellow workers gave it to me after . . . as a kind of honor, you know . . ." He was embarrassed, ashamed to be presenting his daughter with such a bizarre object.

Genia turned it over in her hand. A chunk of metal with a rod extending from it. She looked at her father and his eyes seemed to be imploring her. She placed the object on the table, turned to him, and kissed his cheek.

"Thank you, my beauty," he said, reaching out to embrace her.

"I have to go to school now."

"Yes. We'll have your party tonight. Thank you."

She ran from the kitchen, waving when she reached the door. A few minutes later she was back, picked up the machine part from the table, and placed it in her schoolbag. Then she ran out again and her father remained gazing out after her a long time, absentmindedly plucking at the rose blouse with his thick fingers.

The girls arrived in the evening, both wearing the stockings Genia had given them earlier, in school. She'd shown her friends how to secure them by twisting the top of the nylon around a coin, a kopeck, until it formed a taut band on the thigh.

Each girl handed Genia a gift as she entered. From Vera, a book with pictures of wildflowers. From Mariusha, a small bottle of cologne. The scent was harsh and overly sweet, intended to mask odors, not at all like the subtle fragrance her mother used to wear. But Genia kissed Mariusha and led her to the sitting room.

"This is my father, Giorgi Mikhailovitch," she said. Though their parents knew each other, Mariusha had never been to the house before.

Mariusha didn't flinch, and Vera greeted Giorgi as though they were old acquaintances. Genia wondered at it. He looked as he always did, with a frightening mask for a face. Could it be, she thought vaguely, that her friends forgave his looks because she did?

When Dmitri came down, Vera turned pink. She took his hand and held on as though she never intended to let go. "Those dreadful horses," she murmured, looking into his eyes instead of at his foot. "Genia told me . . ."

"Vera Ivanova," he replied with a smile, "if the horses cause you concern, I'll never go near another one."

Vera batted her lashes. Genia noticed that her large breasts were outlined against her cotton shirt. "This is my friend Mariusha," she said, introducing her to Dmitri in a tone of annoyance.

"I am very pleased to make your acquaintance," he told Mariusha, a blond, vivacious girl whose small nose she referred to as her "snout."

Dmitri was charming tonight, Genia thought, and very handsome in his black shirt, which made him seem even paler than he was, like a poet.

Genia wore her new blouse from her father and the skirt Aunt Katya had made for her: white violets on a field of dark blue. She'd brushed her hair vigorously and it shone, falling loose and thick to her shoulders. She felt beautiful and happy.

The evening was more harmonious than she had dared to imagine.

All of them drank wine, even Aunty Katya, who ordinarily spoke darkly of "the grape and the grain." She seemed carefree tonight, flushing with pleasure when the others cleaned their plates and even accepted second helpings. She was wearing her best dress, Genia saw, a flowered print with flounces at the sleeves, and her chain of amber beads with the silver clasp.

At the meal's end, Katya brought in the cake and placed it before Genia. "May all the surprises in your life be happy ones," she said, handing her the knife.

Genia cut into it, unsuspecting. Inside the cake was pale ice cream studded with small nuggets of colorful frozen fruit. Genia grinned. "This is the best birthday of my life," she said.

But as she was hugging Katya, Genia thought of her birthday the year before. Her mother had worn a red dress with a flaring skirt, and when she danced, the skirt flew up above her knees, but she went on dancing, not caring if anyone saw, twirling faster and faster as the skirt circled around her, revealing her thighs, and Natasha's head was thrown back as her laughter filled the room and her bright skirt went on spinning.

Genia caught Dmitri's eye and knew he was remembering too.

After the cake, Giorgi put a record on the phonograph, the Red Army Chorus singing the best-loved Russian folk songs, and when they began "Krasavitzsa Maya," he sang along boisterously, looking at Genia. *"Ti pastoy, pasto-o-o-oy, krasavitzsa maya . . .* You must wait, wait, my beauty . . ."

The others joined in. The love song had been composed by a Russian soldier to his sweetheart as he was leaving for war. *"Dozdval na' gladeztva/ Radozt na tibya . . .* Until I come back to my happiness with you . . ." Dmitri moved closer to Vera and put an arm around her shoulder.

"My son," Giorgi called over to him when the song ended, "remember last year, on Genia's birthday? We danced together like two Cossacks."

They'd danced with arms around each other, deep on their haunches, kicking up their heels. That was before everything, Genia thought. Even before their quarrel, in a time of peace.

"I remember," Dmitri said. He withdrew his arm from Vera, and no one spoke for a few minutes, as a pall settled over their gaiety. "You'll dance again," Vera said finally, turning to Dmitri. "Miracles can happen."

He tried to smile back, but his face was grim.

Genia looked at her friends helplessly. The joy of the party was over.

Ever since Genia could remember, the family had spent two weeks each summer at their dacha, the lakeside country house they'd been awarded (like the Zil limousine) as a perquisite of her father's position. This year Dmitri would be on crutches, and Genia wondered if he'd be able to swim with her across the lake.

But when the time came to leave the city, Dmitri announced he wasn't going.

Aunt Katya looked at him in alarm, unsure whether she should continue packing his shirts in the suitcase. "Impossible," she said, and took another shirt out of his drawer to fold.

"Stop that," Dmitri ordered. "I told you I won't go."

To Katya, life moved on a fixed, orderly course. Breaking with routine was an invitation to chaos. She put the shirt back and hastened out to inform his father.

Within minutes Giorgi was stomping into Dmitri's room. "What do you mean, not going?" he shouted.

"I prefer to stay here and continue with my studies," his son answered coolly, though a waver in his voice betrayed agitation. Dmitri had not been able to attend school since his accident, but had studied hard at home and had come out third in his class at the end of the school year. After that he'd continued studying on his own.

"You're going, I tell you!"

"To do what? Engage in sports? Make small talk with the elitist neighbors? No, I'm staying here."

"You can*not*. There's no one to cook for you." In his anger, Giorgi seized on the first practical obstacle.

"I'll cook for myself, as other people do. I don't need anyone waiting on me. I don't need a dacha either. How many citizens have a dacha?" His voice was becoming impassioned. From her side of the partition, Genia heard the danger signs and shut her eyes tight to squeeze out their quarrel.

"Dacha be damned!" Dmitri was shouting. "Special privilege sets up elitism, the curse of the managerial class, which threatens the true meaning—"

"Enough!" Giorgi bellowed. "You have all the answers, don't you? At sixteen. I tell you you are ignorant. You talk about socialism and haven't understood its first rule, which is to recognize authority and obey it. You'll come to no good, I can promise you. You defy your father, you spurn authority—and you will be cast off, you'll become one of the drifters and malingerers who infect our society until we cut them out!"

"As you did to my mother."

A dreadful silence followed. Genia was trembling on the other side of the wall. She heard her father say slowly and clearly: "I wash my hands of you." And then she heard the stomp of his uneven footsteps as he walked out of Dmitri's room, and the familiar sickness came back to her stomach.

Next morning she sat stiffly between her father and Aunt Katya and spoke to neither of them during the entire ride out to the country.

But once at the dacha, she began to relax. She swam in the lake every day, not as far out as she would have swum with Dmitri, closer to the shore, but she swam at least an hour a day in two, sometimes three separate swims, always alone, her troubles floating away in the rhythm of her strokes.

Midmorning or early afternoon she took walks with her father, and found she enjoyed them despite his slow pace. There was no tension between them. They commented on plants and trees as they passed, or he pointed out birds flying overhead and named them for her. Sometimes they walked in silence, but they were comfortable with each other. Usually Genia picked flowers on their walks and arranged them in artistic bouquets when they were back at the house.

They were always alone when they walked through the woods and across fields. By the fifth day Giorgi began telling his daughter stories from his boyhood and about his parents— her grandparents—about whom she hadn't heard before.

At night they played cards together, or he read aloud to her from Pushkin and from modern novelists like Alexei Tolstoy. While he read, he drank only water, and though no day went by without his consuming a half-liter or more of vodka, it seemed to make him mellow in the country, not wild with grief or rage.

The days were peaceful and Genia was content. But if her mind went back to other summers when they'd all been a

family together, she became disconsolate and lonely. She tried
to block her memories and not to think about Dmitri, whom
she was missing badly. She never mentioned him, or her
mother, to Giorgi.

But on the ninth day of their stay, when it had been raining
without stop for thirty-six hours, Genia had become so restless
that without thinking, she said aloud: "I wish Dmitri were
here."

Her father stopped rocking in his chair, and put down his
copy of *Pravda*. She wanted to bite her tongue.

"I wish so too," he said.

"You do?"

"My son and I, we're knitted of the same wool," he said
reflectively. "I see myself when I look at him, as I used to
be. . . ."

"But the two of you argue so terribly!"

Giorgi nodded. "Yes. People who are most alike fight each
other the most viciously. Two cats in a fight are more ferocious
than a cat and dog." He picked up the paper from his lap, and
Genia looked out behind him at the dark gray sheet of water
beating against the glass.

Giorgi held his paper to one side. "History is full of
examples," he went on, "to show that a family can be more
murderous than strangers."

"Do you love Dmitri?"

He gave her a strange look. "How can I? He is myself."

He went back to his *Pravda* again and Genia stared blankly
at the sheet of water as his words echoed in her thoughts. She
didn't understand how a handsome young man like Dmitri
could be the same as her father. They looked as different as
night and day, or sunshine and storm. She tried picturing them
with transposed faces, her brother disfigured, her father
handsome. But it was useless, impossible to get an image. All
she could picture was a young man, her father as a boy, and
pretend that he still existed, somewhere inside Giorgi,
struggling to come out but constantly repelled.

When they returned from the dacha, Dmitri looked thinner.
He welcomed Aunt Katya with relief and seemed bursting to
tell his sister about what he'd read and learned in her absence.
To his father he was impersonal but polite, and for the rest of
the summer the two avoided further confrontations.

Genia went back to the Pioneers, helping to get the nursery ready for its opening in the fall. When she wasn't working, she visited Mariusha, now her best friend. Genia had decided that Vera was basically frivolous, a decision that had come at the time of Genia's discovery that Dmitri was interested in her friend.

Vera was the first person he went to visit when he switched from crutches to a cane. Dmitri found her charming and original, with a good mind despite her youth, and possessing an artistic flair like his mother. In addition, her body was ripe beyond its years and she was half Jewish, like himself. A girl made for him.

He wanted to be healthy and strong again so he could dance with her, lift her above his shoulders, carry her in his arms without limping. Perhaps, he thought, looking at the flowered cotton that clung to her rounded hips, he'd been too hasty in refusing the American's offer. Bernard Merritt's "friends" might be able to restore him, replace his limping gait with a manly stride. He owed that to Vera, he rationalized, not to mention society itself, which required able-bodied citizens to carry out its aims.

But when Bernard next came to the house, at the end of September, Dmitri was at school and missed his visit.

Bernard came in the middle of the day, on an urgent mission to warn Giorgi of impending changes in Party leadership. Rumors in the West suggested that Marshal Zhukov, hero of World War II, would be deposed soon, perhaps imminently.

"Malicious rumors," Giorgi replied. But a chill ran through him and he felt pain in the missing joints of his fingers.

"Giorgi Mikhailovitch," Bernard addressed him curtly, "I don't have time for meaningless refutations. I've come here at some risk to myself, and I don't intend to waste these minutes listening to you parrot the Party line."

"You will not speak to me like that in my own house!" Giorgi's skin was blotched with anger.

"It may not be yours for long. You must listen to me, I beg you." He stood facing his host in the center of the sitting room, having refused to take even a cup of tea in order not to waste a moment.

"What's your motive?" Giorgi asked bluntly. "Don't tell me you came to warn me for the sake of our 'friendship.'"

"As it happens, I do have friendly feelings for you, but you know the answer to your question. I've committed myself deeply to the farm deal and I expect it to go through. I also expect to be recompensed according to the terms we agreed on. Clear enough?"

"Indeed. Your 'friendly feelings' arise from your lust for acquisition."

"What good is this bickering? Neither of us wants the deal to fall into the wrong hands. At best, you stand to be tried on criminal charges for theft of the ikons. Or you could vanish without a trace, if my loan is interpreted as a bribe. It would mean you've abused your position in the Party and have betrayed your country by working in the pay of Western imperialists."

His hands behind his back, his mutilated fingers aching painfully, Giorgi paced up and down the room, from window to fireplace and back again. "And you? You're discredited by *your* government. You've lost the contract—not to mention the priceless treasures you intend to keep for yourself."

"Right," Bernard agreed easily. "And now that we've both said what each of us already knows, can we get back to the point? Time's wasting."

"I admit . . ." Giorgi began, and stopped pacing so close to Bernard that the American stepped back instinctively. "I myself have had suspicions recently . . . though I couldn't verify them. I've taken some steps already. Don't ask what they are—it's not in your interest." Giorgi prodded Bernard on the chest. "All I will tell you is that my precautions will keep the deal viable even if . . . if something should happen to me. It's a minor protection for myself, yes, but of major benefit to you. Remember the word 'Lotko'—never mind what it means . . . nothing, really—and be prepared for shipments."

Bernard touched Giorgi's shoulder lightly. "I apologize for underestimating you. I'm grateful. Very grateful. Can I do anything for you in return?"

Giorgi sucked in his breath, held it a moment, and then spoke rapidly: "If it should come about, I beg you to protect my children. It would be for a short time only, a few months or so. I estimate that the present strategy is, in the main, an elaborate window dressing. The policy against 'international-ism' is a calculated reaction to the Yugoslav situation, a temporary move. It means denouncing all ties with the West and rounding up anyone known or suspected to have been friendly with Westerners. As I see it, I'll be removed from my post and possibly from Leningrad itself—but only temporarily.

When Yugoslavia is 'normalized,' I'll be quietly slipped back to my old position.

"But in the meantime, all will proceed *as though* I were being removed permanently, as an example to others against fraternizing with the West. My children will be decreed orphans and may become wards of the state." He stopped, drew in his breath again, and taking both Bernard's hands in his, implored him: "Look after my children. Protect them. I beg it of you, Bernard."

It was too sudden, unexpected. Even Bernard's quick grasp of situations faltered before the implications of Giorgi's plea. Stalling for time, he said: "Dmitri would never accept me as a protector."

"He may have to."

"He's sixteen, isn't he? Maybe old enough for the state to leave him alone."

"Maybe. But Genia's only thirteen. A young girl. She needs someone to look after her. And she's fond of you."

Bernard pictured her as she'd been one night at dinner, attacking her food with lusty appetite, her red-gold hair gleaming, her eyes bright with vivacity. And when he'd given her the stockings—such a simple gift!—she'd run up and kissed him. "I'm fond of her . . ." He faltered, and his fears suddenly blurted out: "I've never had children! I don't know them."

Giorgi was eyeing him, Bernard felt, almost with pity. "Nevertheless," said Giorgi in a calm, even assured voice, "you must do what you can."

The decision seemed to have been made without Bernard's conscious consent. He could not remember anything like this happening to him before.

"You may have to take them out of the country," Giorgi went on.

"Smuggle them out?" For a moment Bernard was exhilarated by the idea. A daring act. A challenge. Then he thought of the next step. "Suppose you're detained longer than you anticipate? What if you're exiled for a year, even more?"

"That's unlikely."

"And if it happens nonetheless?"

"I have no one else to turn to," Giorgi said simply. "The ikons will start arriving within weeks of my arrest, should it take place. The boxes will be postmarked from Canada, and will contain foodstuffs or textiles. Each box will have one hollow side."

"The ikon?"

"Yes."

"'Lotko' is my reference?"

"Yes. You'll receive the St. George, the Rose Madonna, and the Emerald Cross."

"The Emerald Cross?" More than he'd hoped for, worth at least a million at open auction, though Bernard would never sell.

"For the children. Or for Genia, at least." Giorgi went to the cabinet and poured each of them a snifter of brandy. As he held out Bernard's glass, he said nonchalantly, "As her guardian, you'll be reimbursed for as long as I'm in exile, as long as I remain alive. I am arranging now to 'transfer' the Kiev Virgin to you."

Bernard's hand was shaking as he took the brandy. The Kiev Virgin with her mysterious smile was the *Mona Lisa* of Russian ikons, the most valuable of all.

Giorgi was watching his face. "I see my proposal appeals to you." He held out his glass.

Bernard lifted his and clicked with Giorgi's. "It's a deal."

Shortly after Bernard's visit, though the children didn't know it had taken place, things began to change at home. Dmitri noticed it first: his father's distracted state of mind, the sound of his heavy footsteps pacing at night, a tension in the air. He said nothing to Genia, in order not to alarm her. And besides, there was nothing specific to tell. But the sense of things being out of balance continued. Dmitri could feel it pervading the house, something infiltrating the rooms, vague but ominous.

And one evening three weeks later Genia came home in tears because Mariusha's parents hadn't permitted her to come into their apartment to visit their daughter. They'd whispered hurriedly that she was not to come back again, and begged her to forgive them, saying they had no choice.

From then on Genia, too, was aware of something moving through the house. She was afraid to sleep because of nightmares.

In the last week of November they were wakened by a sharp knock on the door, followed by a barrage of rapping and shouting. Genia ran out to the hallway. Dmitri and Aunt Katya were already there, holding each other's hands. Her father was dressed in his street clothes.

"Stay here," he told them sternly. "Whatever happens, stay where you are."

They heard the door being forced open with a crash. A harsh voice shouted up, "Giorgi Mikhailovitch Sareyov?"

"You know damn well it's me," he shouted back. "There was no need to break the door." He began walking down the stairs slowly, holding himself erect in his old military bearing.

When he was halfway down, they couldn't see him anymore. They heard the same voice as before saying, "I am under orders . . ."

And then nothing except the sound of the heavy door groaning on its broken hinges.

After ten days of Bernard's continual efforts, channels were opened wide enough to permit a train ride for Genia to the West.

As Bernard had predicted, Dmitri refused to go. His reasons were both political and sentimental. He would be a stranger anywhere but in his homeland, he told Bernard, and would consider himself a coward if he fled to the West. Leningrad meant engagement, to society and to Vera. The Malchikoffs, her parents, had offered him a bed in their small apartment, in case he and Katya were ejected from their house.

Aunt Katya's future was undecided. She wept almost continuously from the time of her employer's arrest. She wept for herself, for the children, for the terrible affliction of her country since the banishment of God.

Dmitri tried to comfort his sister. He said Bernard had everything to offer her. He reminded Genia how fascinated she'd been on meeting him, and assured her she would come to love her benefactor.

"I don't want to go," she sobbed, clinging to her brother. "You're all I have. I don't want to leave you! I won't!"

He cuddled her on his lap as though she were a baby, and it took all his will not to weep along with her. But Dmitri knew he was unable to keep her with him, and also that he could never leave his country. "We have no choice," he said gently, stroking her hair and willing his fingers to remember the touch.

On the morning of December 8, 1957, she boarded the train for Finland, carrying all her possessions in two small suitcases and her emigration papers in a cotton handbag fastened by a string.

It was snowing heavily when the train began to pull from the station. Within seconds she could no longer see Dmitri and Katya on the platform. Everything was white, blinding her. No forms, no landmarks, nothing but the shifting snow and her own sobs as the wheels gathered momentum.

5

Once beyond the lights of the station, the train plunged through dark clouds of swirling snow. In this, the darkest time of year, day and night merged in the grim twilight of winter solstice at the sixtieth parallel. In December, people stayed indoors, kept the lights on and the fire going, as they withdrew into themselves for annual hibernation. The month of suicide, drunkenness, and domestic violence. That was the true north: the earth's upper region of seasonal extremes and contradictory personalities. On the white nights of June Leningraders danced and embraced in the streets at three in the morning. But the black days of December kept them hidden away from each other.

Genia was alone in her compartment and, for all she knew, in the train itself. The overhead light was harsh and yellow, with no switch to turn it off. There was no knob, either, to turn down the volume of the lugubrious music that flooded the compartment. She felt like a prisoner in a cell, exiled from home.

The train sped north to Finland. After less than two hours, it slowed to its first stop, the station name posted in Cyrillic and Roman letters: ВЫБОРГ , Vyborg. An hour after that, the train stopped again. An official pulled open the compartment doors and asked Genia for her papers. Terrified, she handed them to him without looking up.

"You will step out, please. Leave your luggage here."

"What's wrong? What did I . . . ?"

"We change the wheels," he told her mysteriously, and disappeared, taking her papers with him.

Out the window, Genia saw the name of the station, in Roman letters only: Vaalimaa. She was in Finland now, in the West. She'd left her country and her alphabet behind.

Passengers were stepping off the train, onto the platform. But they seemed relaxed; some were even smiling. She waited in her seat by the window, uncertain what to do next.

"Please." The same official had returned, and he spoke to her more sternly than before. "You will get off the train now." He waited until she stood up.

Genia walked along the corridor and down the steps, clutching her handbag in both hands. What had he done with her papers? What would happen to her? She was shivering, despite her warm coat and the thick boots that protected her from the deep slush on the platform.

"*Hej!* Little girl, you want some tea?" A stocky woman held out a cup, smiling at Genia. She spoke Russian with a strong accent.

Genia tried to smile back, but her face contorted as though she were about to cry.

The woman patted her shoulder, placing the cup in her hands. "Take this. There's always a long wait at the border. Four hours at least. I know, I've come this way often before to visit my sister in Novgorod. She married a Russian engineer. They have two children . . ."

"Please. Why four hours?"

"Because you Russians live in another world, you're still in the nineteenth century," she answered, laughing. "Your tracks are too wide. Your gauge is broader than the rest of Europe's. It takes time to put you on the right track!" She chuckled at her joke. "There, you can see it. Look!"

Genia watched in amazement as a large crane lifted the railroad car up from its wheels. The wheels were shuttled out from underneath the dangling car and a narrower set was slid in place on the inner gauge. The crane then lowered the car onto the new wheels.

The procedure was repeated with each of the railroad cars. When the passengers were permitted to board again, it was late afternoon, dark as night. The Finnish woman joined Genia in her compartment and introduced herself: "My name is Ulla Vitkus. You may call me Ulla."

Ulla glanced at the window as the train began moving and reached forward to pull down the shade. "Nothing to see out there," she said.

"No!" Genia's cry was so vehement that Ulla stopped, hand in midair.

"What's wrong?"

"Please," Genia begged. She felt foolish, but she was afraid of being sealed in, losing her last opening, as it seemed, to the outside world.

"As you like." Ulla shrugged and sat down. She brought out a box filled with iced cakes her sister had baked and offered them to Genia, as the Finnish immigration official came in to return travel documents.

"My ticket is for another car," Ulla told him, holding out the cakes. "But I decided to sit here instead and keep my young friend company."

Genia waited for the tongue-lashing he was about to give the woman, but instead the man smiled, accepted one of the cakes, and asked Ulla's name. After only a moment's search among the papers he was holding, he extracted her passport and returned it to her, at the same time giving Genia back her documents.

"How is it possible?" Genia asked when he'd gone.

Ulla understood the question immediately. She was familiar with the ways of Soviet officials. "We move freely here. In Finland no one needs a special visa to go from one town to another, as in your country. We travel where we like, whenever we want to. And we can change our seats if we please."

A new world. Ulla went on explaining how things were done in her country and Genia listened as though to fairy tales. In Finland, Ulla said, newspapers could criticize the government and the Finnish people were free to demonstrate against official policies. Ulla then asked Genia how long she would be staying in Finland.

"I don't know." Her destination was Helsingfors, Helsinki, where she was to stay with a couple named Krukkala for an indefinite amount of time. Days? Weeks? Maybe more, living among strangers in a strange land. She was an orphan, her family lost to her, and Bernard Merritt only a shadowy figure at the end of an uncharted journey. She felt herself cast adrift, like a traveller in space.

"The Krukkalas?" Ulla asked with interest. "I know them, Olaf and Minna. Everyone in Helsingfors knows of Olaf Krukkala. He was a hero in the resistance against the Russians during the war. He trades with them now!" She chuckled. "War makes nonsense of everything, isn't it so?"

Genia nodded. It hadn't occurred to her that other nations had fought in the war. She'd somehow thought it was only the Russians against the Nazis. Maybe Finnish people had been disfigured by the war too.

"His wife, Minna, writes children's books—in Finnish, for a change, instead of Swedish. The Swedish-speaking Finns run our country," she explained with bitterness. "They consider themselves superior."

Genia stared out at the rushing darkness and felt helpless, already left out of the world she was about to enter.

As if reading her thoughts, Ulla said: "We are a very small country. Everyone knows everyone, and the Krukkalas are excellent people. I'm sure you'll be happy."

When Genia stepped off the train, she was met by two armed soldiers who spoke in strange syllables that didn't sound like a human language. One of them took her bags, and she understood she was to go with them. She looked around for escape, but there was none. Her friend Ulla had said good-bye in the compartment, and was now many meters ahead of Genia, rushing toward a bearded man in a fur hat.

Genia walked between the soldiers. They were taking her to prison, to labor camp, to some place of terrible punishment intended for girls whose parents were enemies of the state. Why hadn't she stayed with Dmitri? Where was Bernard Merritt? Would anyone tell her what she was accused of? Or was it to be like the nighttime arrest of her father, without reason or explanation?

The soldiers escorted her to a room where a group of people seemed to be waiting for her. They smiled as she entered. A large woman with a square, broad face, hair pulled back into a bun, put her arm around Genia's waist. "I'm Minna Krukkala," she said in Russian, leading Genia to a long table where men sat with papers in front of them. A tall rangy man stood at the side. "This is Olaf, my husband."

His reddish-blond hair, much lighter than Genia's, retreated from his scalp and grew in long tufts over his ears. He reached out his hand, but when she didn't respond he stepped forward and embraced Genia. "We're happy you could come to us. I represent Bernard Merritt's concerns in Finland. He sends you a big welcome and hopes to visit you here very soon."

The soldiers left. The immigration formalities were taken care of in a few minutes, and the Krukkalas led Genia out of the station to their car.

She sat in front, between Olaf and Minna, who was driving. She wondered why, if the Krukkalas were entitled to a car this size, they didn't have a driver.

Why were so many cars on the road? The questions hammered dully at Genia, but she didn't ask any of them as they drove through the dark snowy streets. The snow had stopped falling, but the downy softness rested on roofs and branches, in gently peaked mounds on the lampposts, and the sparkle of the snow was caught in the beams of electric light, like at home.

They drove past the harbor. Helsinki was built along the shores of the Gulf of Finland, like Leningrad.

When they arrived at the Krukkalas' house, Olaf went into the kitchen and brought out his bottle of vodka from the pantry, like her father did.

But it wasn't the same at all. Genia sat at the kitchen table with them, a bowl of steaming fish soup in front of her. Olaf's eyes were nearly as light as his hair. His eyebrows were pale and bushy. They moved up and down as he told Genia that Bernard had already phoned to make sure everything was going smoothly. He was obviously very fond of little Genia, Olaf said, and hoped she would be happy during her stay in the West.

Minna said that maybe in a few days they'd go up to their house in the woods for a little skiing.

Genia set her soup to the side. She put her head on her arms and wept.

But as the days went on, the Krukkalas charmed her out of despair. Minna was different from anyone Genia had met, eccentric and humorous, always finding something to laugh about. She called Genia "my potato," and taught her how to make *fil*, the Finnish yogurt, lining up the pots on the window ledge until they set. When a storm destroyed the *fil*— electrical charges in the air causing it to curdle—Minna laughed, saying that with all the secrets in heaven, no one up there knew how to make *fil*, and from time to time the heavens flew into a jealous rage and made all the *fil* in Finland turn bad.

The storm had raged for five hours. "You mean, it was all because of our pots?" Genia asked.

"That's right," Minna told her. "You see how easy it is to control the heavens."

Genia didn't believe her, of course, but she liked Minna's way of making everything human. It was no wonder she wrote books for children: in Minna's world even little people were powerful and could make anything happen.

The Krukkalas bought skis for Genia, long narrow slats of wood with upturned tips, and she learned to race them weekends, when they went to the house in the woods, only an hour's drive from the city. Genia loved their arrival Friday evenings, when they lit the fires and set the big iron pot going on the stove.

They spent Christmas there, a holiday unfamiliar to Genia. She and Olaf went out on snowshoes, Olaf carrying a large ax and evaluating the trees as if he were a judge in a beauty contest: "too stringy," "too short," "good height, but scrawny in the neck." He stopped in front of a blue-gray spruce, an arm's length taller than himself. "Here she is," he exclaimed. "The winner!" He blew the tree a kiss and began to chop it down.

Together they dragged it home, where Minna was busy in the kitchen placing raisins in the eyes of cookie men and women. When she'd finished, the three of them set up the tree in the front room near the fireplace. They placed white candles at the tips of the branches and lit them with long wooden matches. The candle flames winked like stars and the thick branches were pearly in the light. The smell of the tree filled the house.

On Christmas Eve, Genia received presents from Olaf and Minna, gifts they had made for her by hand. A knitted shawl, mittens, a wooden box with her initials etched on the lid—for "secret treasures," Minna said—a flat wooden puppet with a string that made the puppet's limbs jerk up when she pulled. Bernard had sent her a fur jacket, which lay under the tree with the other presents. It was magnificent: soft and white as *fil*, a covering for a snow princess. Genia was delighted by the fur, but embarrassed, too, by its extravagance. She herself had no presents to give, hadn't known that Christmas was a time when people gave things to each other.

They sat down to a festive dinner of smoked salmon and reindeer meat, and after the Christmas cookies and the strong coffee, they raised their glasses to one another and to Bernard in his absence, sipping a liqueur made from Arctic berries.

At midnight the phone rang, and it was Bernard himself, calling to wish them a Merry Christmas. Genia had spoken to him twice before, and each time his voice had sounded disembodied, its stilted Russian seeming to come from a phonograph. "Are you happy, Genia?" he asked now.

"Yes," she said to the strange voice.

"I'll be over to visit you as soon as I can make it."

"Thank you very much." She couldn't quite believe that a real person was at the other end of the telephone, somewhere in America, but she blurted into the receiver, "My father—have you heard from him?"

"I'm sure he's all right, dear girl."

"And my brother . . . ?"

But there was no answer. He'd repeated "Merry Christmas" before the line went dead.

"Don't worry," said Minna, taking the phone from Genia and tousling her hair. "You'll see your fairy godfather very soon."

He arrived ten days later, but had no time, Minna reported, to spend a weekend with them in the country. Genia was disappointed. She was even more disappointed when she heard they'd all be having dinner together at his hotel, the four of them.

In the three weeks since she'd left home, Genia had often imagined her reunion with Bernard. They were alone in a great room, probably a ballroom, of white and gold. He would be waiting for her, and when she came in he would rise, his eyes would light up, and she would float across the floor to his arms and music would begin playing and they would dance, her full skirt rising up as he spun her around and they laughed into each other's eyes.

Instead, she walked into a hotel restaurant designed like a large sauna, its walls lined with flattened beams of bleached wood. Her skirt was not for dancing: a straight tartan ending just below the knees to meet the tops of her thick wool stockings. She was holding Minna's hand, and despite her fur jacket, Genia felt she looked like a child.

Bernard was seated already, across the room from where they entered. His silver hair gleamed. His face was tanned, as she remembered it. He looked like a sea captain, in his navy blazer and white shirt. When they came up to his table, Genia pulled away from Minna. Bernard rose, and Genia waited for his blue eyes to light on her, lift her up—but first he greeted Olaf and kissed Minna's hand.

Only then did he seem to notice her. The marbled sky of his eyes captured her. She blushed as he put his arm around her, drew her against him a moment, then gently pushed her to arm's length so he could study her.

The inspection was brief. He smiled and asked her to sit down beside him on the upholstered bench.

"You look happy," he stated, and she nodded, even though she knew it wasn't a question.

He had decreed that she be happy, and when Genia was seated next to him, his eyes still smiling into hers, she felt she'd been childish in her doubts of him and in her fears that he wouldn't come.

"I'll tell you all my news in a few minutes," he whispered to her. "After we've ordered our meal."

She looked at him with complete trust, and he turned his eyes away from her expression.

A man in evening dress was standing beside Bernard, leaning slightly toward him. Bernard nodded. "Drinks," he said. "What's your pleasure, Minna?"

When it came to Genia's turn, he ordered for her, and the same man in evening clothes returned with a tall glass of dark, bubbling liquid. She tried it. Sweet. She sipped again. "You like it?" Bernard asked.

She shook her head up and down with emphasis, not yet able to unlock her words. "It's called 'Coca-Cola,'" he said, "or 'Coke' for short. The favorite drink of Americans, and you can get it all over Europe now too. We're hoping to bring it to the Soviet Union one day. Think it would sell?"

Again she nodded vigorously, thrilled at being asked her opinion on such matters. The drink was delicious. The formal gentleman and others dressed like him were all waiters, she realized. Genia had been in restaurants before, but when the waiter brought the menu she thought it must be a listing of all foods available in the country.

Bernard leaned toward her and asked, "Would you like help in your selection?"

Amazement restored her speech. "Please," she said, "which of the dishes are available?"

"All of them." The adults were smiling, and Genia smiled

with them. She knew it couldn't be true. Leningrad restaurants had much smaller selections, and never more than two or three were actually available.

But the waiter wrote down their orders. Not once did he say what all Russian waiters repeated to customers after every choice: "Not today." Genia asked Bernard to decide; it was impossible for her.

"A little steak? Good, we'll have the filet mignon," he told the waiter in English. "How do you like it, Genia?"

"Very much," she answered politely.

"No, no"—he was laughing—"I mean, do you like it well done? Rare? Something in between?"

"I like it as it comes," she answered. In a restaurant food came as it did, like milk from a cow or fruit from a tree.

"We'll have it medium-rare," he told the waiter. "And the wine list, please."

Genia had never known that choosing what to eat and drink could involve so many complicated decisions. Bernard showed her the list of wines, page after page in a large leather-bound book, but Genia couldn't understand the reason for it. Wine was wine. Either it was French (her father received a shipment every year) or Soviet. If Soviet, it was either #1, #2, or #3, meaning, as her father had explained, Good, Not So Good, and Barely Drinkable.

Bernard chose something called 157. The waiter went away, pleased by their choices, it seemed—she hadn't seen a waiter smile before—and Bernard put his hand on Genia's. "Now," he said.

She looked at him questioningly. He turned until he was at an angle where he could address all three of them. "First things first. As you know, Genia"—but he looked at Minna—"I made an agreement with your father to bring you to the West. For a short time, to protect you while his 'problems' are being worked out. As of now, it's much too soon to know anything, or even to make a reasonable prediction about his possible release date. We've had no definite news of him, I'm afraid." He spoke as though conferring with someone on important business.

"Your brother seems to be doing fine at the moment. The official order to evict him and the housekeeper is being held up through some kind of bureaucratic muddle. Let's hope for his sake the muddle continues."

"He's *home*? With Aunt Katya?"

"For the moment he is."

"But . . ." She stopped. It might be rude to say, after everything that Bernard and the Krukkalas had done for her. But if Dmitri and Aunt Katya had the house . . .

"He's all right," Bernard was saying. "And we'll continue on the assumption that your father will be reinstated, or at least returned to society, in about six months. Or call it a year, by the most conservative estimate. We've got to have contingency plans just in case."

He was talking to the Krukkalas, not to her. She touched his sleeve. "Am I going home?"

"What do you mean?" Bernard focused on her for the first time since he'd started talking about her family. "We just got you out."

"I mean, the house . . . Dmitri . . ."

"He's fine now," Bernard repeated, saying the words slowly as though she were deaf, "but he may not be next week. Or tomorrow. He has no claim whatever on the property. Genia"—he picked up both her hands—"I promised your father to take good care of you, and that's what I'll do."

"Am I coming to America with you?"

Abruptly, he dropped her hands. "You can't do that. It takes a long time to get the necessary papers, and by the time they came through, your father would be asking for you back. You'll stay with my good friends here for a while longer." He raised his eyebrows in question, looking at the Krukkalas.

Olaf nodded. "A sweet girl."

"She may stay as long as she likes," Minna said. "I've been thinking of making her a heroine in my books. A strong young Russian girl who comes to Finland alone and begins to do wonderful things. Of course she'll have to be a few years younger, closer to my readers' age. But I might make her as old as nine."

"What kind of wonderful things?" Genia asked. As usual, Minna could divert her thoughts from real life to make-believe.

"Magic. She makes cookie people walk and talk, she dives in the lake and comes up with pearls. She rescues a horse from its cruel owner. She mends the broken wing of a bird and it flies again."

"I like that. Will she have my name, your heroine?"

"Of course." When Minna smiled, her broad cheeks seemed to move up toward her eyes. Her skin turned pink as strawberry cream and tiny lines appeared all over her face. Her smile brought on her laughter, which began as a deep rumble and rolled upward through her body, gathering force.

"Good," said Bernard. "I'm glad to see you've made a home here, Genia. Your generosity deserves an ample reward," he said in a lower tone to Olaf, whose ears reddened as he looked away from Bernard.

When the meal ended, Bernard asked Genia to take a short stroll with him. "Why don't you go up to my suite?" he suggested to the Krukkalas, holding out his room key. "There's some good cognac up there, Cuban cigars—help yourselves."

"We'll wait for Genia in the lobby," Minna told him.

"Or perhaps in the bar," her husband added.

"As you like. We'll find you. Can I help you into your jacket, Genia?"

"It's beautiful. Thank you very much for giving it to me."

Bernard smiled and took her arm. "I like giving presents to people who enjoy them," he said.

They went out in the cold night and walked twice around the square, their breaths steaming in front of their faces. It was like walking with her father, almost, her hand nestled in the crook of his arm, matching her step to his. But it was also very different, stepping out after an elegant meal in an elegant restaurant with the most elegant man in the world.

He was hatless, and as they passed under the streetlamps, Genia looked with fascination at his hair, individual strands glistening like metallic threads.

"Whatever you need is yours," he said. Genia remembered Minna calling him her "fairy godfather." "Whatever it is, just let me know, and you'll have it."

She turned her face up to him, but he let his eyes rest on her only an instant. The child's open adoration made him wince.

"I'll do everything in my power," he said, his eyes on the pavement.

"Can you bring my father home?" she asked under her breath, not wanting to tempt the fates.

"That's not in my power," he replied, also softly.

"Can I come and live with you? Please?"

He stiffened, but continued his pace. "I don't have children, Genia. Never had them. Maybe I should have done, when I was younger. But there was always too much else to do, and my wives, well, I never picked one who showed much interest in mothering."

She was flattered. He was speaking to her as a friend, an equal.

"What were they interested in?"

He laughed. The sound wasn't pleasant. "In being Mrs. Merritt. In spending money. Ordering clothes. Being seen. You know."

She didn't.

"What I'm saying is, I don't know children. I don't know how to talk to them or what to do about them. It would be hard for us both if you came to live with me."

"I could teach you how, even though I'm not a child anymore."

He stopped, raised her chin with his forefinger, and kissed the tip of her nose. "That's probably the finest offer I've had, Genia. Thank you."

An hour later, in bed at home, Genia was repeating their conversation to Minna. Minna listened thoughtfully. Then she smiled, but without the tiny lines of laughter. "Bernard Merritt is like a king in a far-off country," she said. "Very powerful and very rich. He rules over many subjects. He owns the most beautiful objects in the world, made of precious stones and precious metals. He is a clever man, and he can read what is written in the hearts of other people. His own heart is made of gold."

"That's nice," said Genia drowsily. She heard what Minna was saying as the beginning of a fairy tale, and not as the warning Minna intended.

Genia remained in Finland with the Krukkalas for five months. Then she was told she had to leave these people who spoke Russian to her and made her part of their family. She couldn't stay in Finland indefinitely, Bernard had told her. She must move westward, must improve her English before she came to him in America.

The excitement of travel, of launching on the long journey to her guardian in New York, was lost on Genia. She'd come to love Olaf and Minna. Her last days in Finland were spent in a kind of mourning for what would take place.

The Krukkalas, too, were depressed at losing Genia. Childless, the couple had kept open a corner of their marriage for a child to enter. Minna had been filling the vacancy with her young heroes and heroines, but when flesh-and-blood

Genia came into the Krukkalas' lives, she occupied the place that had been waiting for her for many years.

The Krukkalas accompanied Genia by ship to Stockholm. There they took a sorrowful leave of each other, though Genia was too numb this time to cry. A Swedish associate of Bernard's put her on the train to Göteborg. She traveled, again by ship, to The Hague.

Holland was her last stop on the continent that connected her with Russia. From there she sailed to England, her entrance to the English-speaking world.

As Giorgi's exile became deeper, surrounded by silence so thick that even Bernard couldn't extract a single piece of news, Bernard had been forced to think about Genia's future. The girl hadn't been to school since December. He couldn't estimate how long she'd be in his charge; all he knew was that her father was still alive. The shipments from Canada had reached Bernard. The Rose Madonna, the St. George, with a note in the shipment of fabrics that "the green check" was on order. That meant the Emerald Cross. And after that, however long it took, *she* would arrive, the Kiev Virgin.

Bernard had to plan for Genia's education. England was an interim step. If any light were thrown on Giorgi's situation, if his release were imminent, Genia would still be in Europe and could be moved back with a minimum of confusion. But if Giorgi remained buried alive somewhere, Genia would have to come to America, where Bernard could supervise her more easily. Over the summer, he could arrange the papers for her while she improved what English she'd learned at school and become more fluent in those few months. She could then enter an American school at the beginning of the academic year.

In England, she lived with people called Plunkett-Jones, business associates of Bernard's, like everyone else she'd met in the West, in a village clotted with roses. The flowers grew everywhere, covering up the entrances and even the entire ground floor of many cottages along the only street of the village, which was named, with spectacular lack of imagination, The Street. Roses bloomed in every color, even striped, and ranged in size from marbles to soccer balls. Their smell permeated the air with cloying sweetness, which Genia hated because it was the smell of decay.

She had no children to play with and no one to talk to,

except her English tutor. The Plunkett-Joneses were often
away in London. At home in Kent, they were busy with their
horses or socializing with neighbors. Genia was lonely, and
withdrew into herself. She had no sense of the country she was
in, only of an opulent garden filled with roses and strangers.
She'd had no direct news from home since leaving Leningrad.
Her letters to Dmitri had all gone unanswered.

In one of his weekly phone calls Bernard told Genia that her
brother had been "relocated," but that so far he'd been unable
to discover Dmitri's new address. Giorgi still had not been
heard from.

The time in Kent passed like a dream, but not a pleasant
one. Genia felt she was treading water to stay afloat. Except for
working on her English, she was barely conscious of anything,
as though she'd just undergone an operation and was now
drifting in and out of drugged sleep, unaware if they were
hours, days, or weeks that were passing.

At the end of August 1958, her tutor brought Genia to
Southampton, where she boarded the SS *United States* to
complete the last phase of her journey across an ocean that
separated her from everything she'd known.

6

Genia stood at the railing in muggy darkness at five in the morning. Daybreak came slowly, a spread of pale gray as the ship inched to shore. The fog was too thick for her to make out the line of horizon between sea and sky, and the air was dense, hot. She had to open her mouth to breathe.

As the mist lightened into morning, other passengers came out on deck, blinking in the hot glare. "It's New York for sure," said one. "A city with air you can see and touch."

The fog lifted suddenly, like a curtain rising on a stage. Cheers went up, people were pointing and calling to each other, "There she is! There's the Lady!" Genia looked out to her left and saw the Statue of Liberty.

She'd seen pictures of it in a book Bernard had given her about New York, and in another book she'd read with her English tutor. The enormous green-patinaed woman with a torch in her upraised hand was supposed to represent freedom and hope for the oppressed. As they sailed past, Genia kept looking at the statue standing alone on her little island, and thought: She's like me.

It was nearly noon when Genia walked down the gangplank, searching for Bernard in the sea of faces on the dock. She stepped off the ramp, onto the hard concrete that represented her first contact with American soil. She didn't see Bernard, but she saw a sign lettered with her name. She walked up to the man who was holding it and said, "I'm Genia."

He brought the sign down and wiped his face with a handkerchief. "Happy to meet you. I'm Mr. Merritt's chauffeur, name's Ross," he said. "Just hand me your baggage tags—good—and stay right where you are. Won't be a moment." He was off, patches of sweat darkening the back of his uniform, and Genia stood by herself, watching the reunions taking place around her, the hugs and kisses, exclamations of joy, children being lifted up in the arms of their fathers.

He hadn't come to welcome her off the ship.

The chauffeur came back surprisingly quickly with her baggage and brought it directly to a customs official. The man smiled at Genia. "Any contraband?"

She didn't know what he meant, and stiffened.

"We'll let it go this time." He winked and waved her off with her bags. "Welcome to New York, honey. You're going to love us."

Ross pushed through the crowd and Genia followed him, out to the most enormous car she'd ever seen, except for those that carried dead officials to their funerals. He held the back door open for her and she went into what seemed a small room, with cozy seats and a bar.

They started moving and Ross's voice came through a small loudspeaker at Genia's side. "Would you like a Coke, Miss Sareyov?"

She shook her head no toward the enclosure where he sat.

"Or something else? Juice? Lemonade? It's all there in the bar in front of you. Just press the silver button."

Like in a fairy tale, but it was eerie. "No, thank you," she said to the emptiness. Why hadn't Bernard come to meet her? Could he be ill? Traveling somewhere, not in America at all?

On either side of her the buildings shot up into the sky, one next to the other, rising to peaks. Skyscrapers, she remembered. But they didn't scrape the sky, they pierced it. Would she be living in one of them? So far off the ground?

People were in a hurry despite the scorching heat; the streets were crowded. Some people carried paper bags. On a bench under a tree, two men were opening their bags. She understood—lunch—and felt relief; there were real people in America after all.

"We're here," said the chauffeur's voice. "Mr. Merritt has a triplex on top."

"Triplex?" she asked when she stepped out. A tall building rose in front of her, but to her right Genia saw trees and grass. A park.

"A three-story apartment, a penthouse. He owns the hotel, you see."

"Hotel?"

"The Hotel François. Main entrance is just around the corner, on Fifth Avenue, but this is Mr. Merritt's private entrance." He led her to it and then, bags under his arms, went into the elevator. There were only two buttons, marked P and L.

"Penthouse and Lobby," said Ross. "Mr. Merritt will give you the key to it."

They rode up and stepped out into a hallway filled with fresh flowers, hung with paintings. The ornately wrought front door opened as she approached and she walked into Bernard's open arms.

"Welcome, dear girl," he said.

"It's you," Genia said in Russian, closing her eyes.

She was taller now, the top of her head coming to nearly the bridge of his nose, but she held it lower, against his neck. "You weren't there. When I came off the ship . . ."

He relaxed his hold, but Genia still clung to him. He patted her back. "I was at the office. Left everything and rushed down here as soon as Ross called me from the car. Come now, Genia," he answered in Russian as he disengaged himself.

Tears stood in her eyes. He hadn't been ill, hadn't been out of the country. Simply busy.

Now he looked at her, holding her at arm's length. "You're thinner, Genia. Are you well?"

She nodded. In England, the only good meal had been breakfast. For the rest of the day, eating wasn't a pleasure.

"Ross will take care of your luggage. You had a good trip? Fine. You'll want to see the apartment right off."

They were standing in the entrance hall behind the front door, a rotunda with a high cupolaed ceiling like Genia's and Dmitri's bedroom at home. A crystal chandelier was suspended from the dome's center, its delicate strings beaded with hundreds of tiny prisms like a web of sparkling raindrops. The floor they were standing on was checkered with black and white marble squares.

Genia didn't care to see the apartment yet. She wanted the familiar welcome a traveler was given at home. When you arrived from a long journey you sat down, drank tea, and talked for a long time. She had many things to ask him. But Bernard was leading her through the first door to the right. It opened on a room that seemed part of a palace or museum. Paintings in heavy gilt frames hung on the walls. The furniture, of polished wood and brocade upholstery, stood on the Persian carpet as though meant for display only, not for use. Bernard pointed out objects on the tables and sideboards. A basket woven of silver reeds, a china vase so sheer it was nearly translucent, a bowl made of hammered gold, set with corals at the rim.

"*Krassnie*," she said to each. "Beautiful."

"This house is full of beautiful things. I've been collecting for most of my life. At first it was anything that took my fancy. Then I began to specialize. I have a few collections now, not all of them important, but substantial. An Oriental collection, impressionists, African art. Most of those I keep in my other houses. Here I keep the finest pieces of all."

They walked into another room, more splendid than the first.

"Here," he pointed to a painting, "is something you should recognize. No? Kandinsky, one of your great masters. My Russian collection spans a thousand years, from ikons to modernist painters, which the Soviets now condemn as 'decadent.'

"I have silver from Ivan the Terrible, a nightstand and several chairs that belonged to Peter the Great. In my library there's a signed volume from Voltaire to Catherine the Great, and several pages of a Tolstoy manuscript. But the ikons, the ikons are what I care most about." He said the last with passion.

Genia looked at this strange man, the sleek American leading her through his palace of Russian treasures.

A person couldn't live in a place like this, she thought miserably. No one would dare to sit on such furniture. And in winter, what did one do with wet boots?

He kept asking for her praise. "Isn't that beautiful?" "What do you think of this"—a small sculpture of a bird—"Magnificent, isn't it? Eight hundred years old." Genia repeated "beautiful" or "wonderful" mechanically, hardly looking at what he pointed out or brought over to her.

They went up the stairs, a curving spiral carpeted in deep

purple. "I'll show you where you'll be staying now. You must be curious."

She wasn't. She wanted to run away from this splendor, this tyranny of things. She wanted to be home or back in Finland. America was too grand. Bernard, walking directly in front of her, seemed at a greater distance than he'd been since she'd met him.

"This is your suite," he said proudly. The bedroom was large, its rounded walls lined in pale linen with tiny cream-colored rosebuds. The bathroom was azure, with a deep blue marbleized tub and a telephone on the wall beside it. Large ferns seemed to grow above the ceiling, their shadows falling on the smoky glass.

Her sitting room was smaller than the bedroom, powder blue, with a blue-rose-and-ocher carpet. "I had it decorated in the style of Versailles," Bernard said, pointing out the delicate table with its narrow legs ending in the splayed feet of a bird. On the table rested a small gold box encrusted with jewels in bright colors. Bernard picked it up. "I put this here especially for you," he said, smiling. "It belonged to the Romanoffs. You can use it for whatever you like. Hairpins, knickknacks."

Genia thought of the wooden box at the bottom of her suitcase, the box Olaf had carved with her initials, for her "treasures."

The Romanoffs. Versailles. A whole apartment for herself. Genia took deep breaths to stop her tears. Like living on a stage set; why couldn't she simply have a room, an ordinary room next to his?

"Beautiful," she forced herself to say.

He pointed out the small kitchen, leading from her hallway, where she could keep drinks in the refrigerator or cook for herself, if she ever wanted to.

Why would she want to? Wasn't she here to live with him? "Won't we . . . you and I . . ."

"Yes?" Bernard waited.

"Eat *together*?" she blurted out.

"Well, my dear. On nights when it's possible, we will. Other nights you might want to eat with Sonya—she's my cook—or take your meal in your apartment."

"Why would I? I've come to live with you."

He still hadn't looked at her in the old way, his eyes passing through hers into what lay behind. "You'll only be here for a little while, Genia, until your father can take you back."

"When will that be?"

"I don't know. Look," he said with a touch of impatience, "you know what the situation is. I've promised your father to take care of you for as long as he's . . . well . . . not in a position to do so himself. All of us expected him to be out by now. So for the time being I'm your guardian, and I'll see to it that you're well taken care of. You'll be going off to school in a few days . . ."

She looked at him in terror. They were still standing in the hallway in front of the small kitchen. Suddenly Bernard softened. He took both of her hands and opened them wide. "I'm sorry. We'll talk about it later." He pulled her close to him, hugged her a moment, and drew away. They started walking slowly out of her apartment. "Please try to understand, Genia. I'm not a parent. I *can't* be."

The tears she'd been holding back rushed down her cheeks.

"Look," he said helplessly. "Genia. Don't cry. Please don't." He waited for her to compose herself. "I *have* to be back at the office this afternoon. Visitors from Saudi Arabia. But later tonight, it'll be just the two of us." He smoothed back her hair, and handed her his white handkerchief. It smelled of lavender, a clean outdoor smell. She gave him a little smile, and blew her nose.

"Good girl." Bernard refused to take back the handkerchief after she'd used it. "It's yours now," he said. "Feeling a little better? Good. Now let's have you meet some of my household staff. They'll help you get organized. How's your English?"

"Middling," she answered, in English.

He smiled. "Very British, that. Classy. I like it."

They spoke English as he introduced her to several servants. But in the kitchen, large as a restaurant and lined with bright tiles—"hand-painted, from Spain. I selected each individually," Bernard told her—they were back to Russian.

"*Eta Gregori*—this is Gregori Leontov." A tall man whose upper body stooped like a scythe, he had a white mustache and small beard. "Gregori is majordomo of the household, in charge of everything. Even me," Bernard said jovially, patting the man's curved back. "He's my valet."

Gregori bent over Genia's hand, his mustache stopping within an inch of it. "*Ochen priatna*, pleased to meet you."

"And this is Sonya, who's in charge of Gregori. She's also the best cook in New York. My favorite woman." He winked at her.

"*Dobro pojzalovatz!* Welcome!" She pumped Genia's hand vigorously in both of hers. "We've been hearing much about you from Bernard Robertovitch, Mr. Merritt, and we've been looking forward to your visit. You and I have much to talk about. I, too, come from *Piter*." Genia recognized the old term for Leningrad when it was St. Petersburg. "The tea is ready. Shall I serve it in the alcove?" Sonya asked Bernard.

"Wherever Genia likes. I have to be running back, I'm afraid."

As if on cue, Ross came into the kitchen. "Ready, Mr. M.?"

"Coming." To Genia he said, "If you want to see more of the house, ask Sonya. She'll take you on a regular Cook's tour." He chuckled. Genia looked at him blankly.

"I'll try not to be too late, though I'll have to stop off at the UN for a reception before dinner. It you need anything, ask Sonya or Gregori. They have my office number if there's anything else. My secretary knows who you are." He gave a little wave and started to leave the kitchen. Suddenly remembering, he turned back, went up to Genia, and kissed her forehead.

He walked away quickly. She stood looking after him, tensed for the sound of the front door closing. But when it came, Genia felt it as a blow to her chest. She grabbed a chair and let herself fall into it, shaking her head when Sonya offered tea.

Sonya looked at the girl, reading the obvious distress on her face. "It will get better," she said gently. "You are feeling homesick. It is natural. When I had to leave Piter I was a younger girl than you are now. I cried and cried! At night, the river Neva flowed through my dreams."

Genia let her head fall onto her arms. The Neva. Home.

"But soon," Sonya reassured her, "you will be happy again. You'll see—after a while you won't even care to go back."

Genia shook her head, but kept it down. If she never went back, she'd remain an orphan all her life. "I don't belong here," she mumbled.

Over the entrance to the Ashe-Willmott School in Regent's Park, Connecticut, the motto stood in darkened bronze: *Veritas Est Fortis*. Truth is strength. Genia glared at the letters as they drove through, up the sweeping roadway to the main building. Sent to prison, she thought, like her father. This would simply be another prison like the palatial one she'd just left, after less than a week. She hated the bushes, the trees, the smooth rolling lawn, the view of the river, and most of all she hated the girls she saw from the car window, in silly trousers that ended above the knee, walking in pairs or little groups, talking and laughing with each other.

Ross went with her to the headmistress's office, and introduced Genia to Miss Willmott. "Thank you," said the gray-haired woman whose voice was like a taut string. "You won't be needed anymore. We'll take care of everything."

Genia squeezed his hand as Ross walked out, wishing he could stay just a little longer.

"Eugenia Sareyov," said Miss Willmott, "you will be an unusual addition to our school. We haven't had a girl from your country before, though some of our girls come from as far away as Argentina. I'm sure you'll feel right at home, and if anything should trouble you, feel free to come in and talk to me about it."

Never, Genia thought, looking at the hard face. With spectacles, it would be the face of the judge who'd sentenced her mother.

An older girl showed Genia to her dorm, the Susan B. Anthony house, a plain-looking wooden building on a hill overlooking the river. Behind the house were tennis courts, and beyond them, the stables. "My name is Leigh," the girl said. "I live in Aphra Behn House—I'm a senior. Susan B. Anthony is for new students, freshmen or transfers. Quite a few foreign girls live here. You'll make friends."

Leigh showed her to her room, small and simply furnished with bed, desk, chair, and dresser. No paintings on the wall. "Do you understand what I'm telling you?" Leigh asked. "Do you speak English?" Her tone was unfriendly.

"A little," Genia answered. Her window looked out on the tennis courts. The curtains were a pale tobacco color.

"You're from Russia, aren't you?" Leigh was studying her as though she were some peculiar being, Genia felt.

"Yes."

"Pretty bad over there, isn't it? Communism."

Genia shrugged.

"You're lucky you got out." Leigh was still scrutinizing her. "You must be very glad to be in the free world."

"Thank you," said Genia, swallowing hard. Her bags had been placed in the center of the room. She pulled one of them on her bed and began unpacking, her back to the American girl.

"Well . . . you have any questions?"

"No. Thank you."

"Guess I'll be going then," she said. "Good luck."

In the next days, Genia took tests to determine where she would be placed academically. Her comprehension of English was excellent, far exceeding her speaking ability. She scored very high on the math and was officially placed in the eleventh year, making her a junior at fourteen and a half, a year younger than the others in her class.

Despite Leigh's prediction, Genia didn't make friends. She didn't dare speak to the long-legged, self-assured girls, whose faces seemed closed to her. And none of the girls made an effort to befriend her. The girl across the hall from her was a Rockefeller. Her neighbor to the right was a Vanderbilt. She recognized the rich, powerful names and withdrew from them.

She could feel their animosity. Conversations stopped as she walked past, and Genia knew the girls had been talking about her. She was an outcast, and felt that to others she was a source of contagion. They saw her as a Communist, carrier of a strange disease which could infect them on first contact. Even the other "foreign" girls stayed away from her. The four who lived in her dorm came from South America, already well-traveled, speaking perfect English. All of them, though strangers to each other, shared an almost obsessive interest in horses.

Dmitri had often accused her of being "politically naive." She'd been a good Pioneer, and the Pioneers were a patriotic organization, but Genia's ideology had been like that of most of her friends. She took it for granted, didn't think about it. She read what she was supposed to and repeated the slogans when they were asked for. A "good" Communist was synonymous to her with a "good" person. And she loved the Pioneers because she had friends there, and they all worked together, building something useful.

Then her parents were arrested, one by one. Genia didn't know and didn't really care about politics. People were people; ideology led to "mistakes" at best (as Dmitri called them). She'd been orphaned, forced to leave her country in the name of "ideology." She loved Russia and the people she knew there. But she had no animosity toward Americans, yet how could she love them if they treated her like a pariah?

She walked alone to her classes, feeling the critical eyes assessing her clothes, her blouses and skirts that marked her as an alien. Though no uniform was prescribed by the school, all the girls wore very short trousers (she had learned they were called Bermudas), usually of madras cotton, boys' shirts, and knee socks. Their hair was worn either in ponytail or pageboy. They all sounded the same when they talked, as though part of their words came through their noses. Genia retreated into solitude and silence.

After three weeks, she was so tired she could barely drag herself to classes. Her head ached, her limbs felt watery. But when Bernard called, as he did every Sunday, she told him she was fine.

"You don't sound it," he said. "You sound like you're down with something, a cold or flu. Look, go on over to the infirmary and have them check you out."

"Yes," she said, "thank you." When she put the phone down, she went back to bed and pulled the covers over her, even though it was a hot, sunny day.

A few minutes later she was wakened by the housemother of the dorm, a stringy young woman whose supposed duty it was to look after the girls as a kind of permanent chaperon, but who rarely came out of her room and didn't yet know all the girls by name. Bending over Genia, she looked worried. "Are you sick?" she asked. "The dean had a call from your guardian."

Genia turned away, but the housemother persisted. She placed a thin, cool hand on Genia's forehead. Then she placed a thermometer under Genia's tongue. When she pulled it out and read it, she whistled softly. "We better get you to the infirmary right away."

She helped Genia dress, packed a small bag of toiletries for her, and guided her over the smooth lawn to the infirmary behind the chapel.

Genia's fever was 104 degrees. She had the Asian flu, and stayed in the infirmary for ten days. Bernard sent roses—a dozen each of orange, deep red, and mauve long-stemmed roses. Genia asked the nurse to take them away—the smell was overpowering, as it had been in England, and the rotting sweetness upset her stomach.

She was alone the first four days, and slept through most of them. On the fifth day, when it was judged that the contagious period was over, Genia was moved into a small ward with four beds, two of them empty.

She woke in the afternoon to see a face peering down with intense concentration. The girl was in a white hospital gown, barefoot, brown hair falling forward as she studied Genia. Noticing Genia's open eyes, she shrank back a little. "You're really beautiful," she said by way of apology. "Hi."

"Hi." The face looking down at her had small eyes, a small nose, and a wide mouth. It was square, the skin dusted with freckles. A pixieish kind of face, Genia thought, friendly and open. Genia smiled.

"You're the Russian, aren't you?"

"It is so."

The girl held out her hand and shook Genia's firmly, like a man. "Lex Vandergrieff. Lex is short for Alexis, and so am I." Her smile lit up the plain face like a sunburst.

Genia sat up and introduced herself.

"I've seen you a few times on campus," Lex said, "and I could tell you were gorgeous. But close up, you're really dynamite!"

Genia laughed. She knew the word "dynamite"; but how could a person be a powerful explosive? Lex's way of talking was very comical.

"How come we never ran into each other before? You live in the infirmary? Are you sick all the time, like those Russian heroines dying of consumption?"

"I am very healthy."

Lex cocked her head and studied her. "You don't look it," she decided.

Genia was used to being scrutinized by the girls, but with Lex it was different. The others looked at her as though she were a blind curiosity who couldn't notice their stares. Lex regarded her with admiration and interest.

"Is what you've got catching?" Before Genia could answer, Lex was sitting on her bed. "Tell me about Russia, the furs, the snow. Everything. How did you get here? How does it feel to be Russian?" Her words gathered momentum as she spoke, snowballing into a large question mark.

"What answer I give?" Genia asked helplessly.

"Tell me about your folks."

"My what?"

"Parents. Your mother and father."

"They are . . . gone."

"Dead?" Lex asked with interest.

"No, away." She didn't want to use the word "prison," or even "exile." What would her new friend think? How could Genia explain?

"What does that mean?" Lex insisted.

"My English is not so good."

Lex looked at her thoughtfully, saw the troubled expression on Genia's face, and asked instead how she had made her way to America.

But over the next days, Genia slowly told the story of her life and Lex listened enthralled, sometimes perplexed, firing a volley of questions whenever Genia paused, until she'd nailed down what Genia was trying to say.

She talked about her parents' arrests and disappearance, about her father's deformity, the loss of her brother, her country—everything. Sometimes her English faltered and wore down. When Genia cried, Lex put her arms around her and rocked her like a little girl. Then Genia would feel her terrible burden starting to lift, the huge, evil bird lessening its hold on her. As she talked—about leaving Russia, the Krukkalas, coming to a guardian who had no time for her—she sometimes felt lighthearted, a brook gurgling under the ice. Feverishness brought vivid images.

Lex's intestinal flu made her leap up, clutching her stomach, and race to the bathroom in the middle of a sentence. But despite their illnesses, the girls talked incessantly, whispering in the dark after lights-out, reaching across the gap between their beds to catch each other's hands when the nurse was coming through to make the rounds.

Amazing, both of them agreed. They were born on opposite sides of the globe, into opposing ideologies, and yet within days—even less—they were as close as sisters. They each felt it, but neither girl understood how it came about.

Born a Vandergrieff, one of America's oldest and wealthiest families, raised with horses, tennis courts, boats, swimming pool, trips to Europe, her own sports car at fifteen, Lex had inherited the fairytale life most girls dreamed about. But what Genia found more wonderful than all the material splendor was Lex's family. It was extensive, with branches reaching across the country, and Lex had a mother and father and an older brother, all of them very close.

Yet somehow Lex was lonely. Lex confided to her new friend that since she'd been very little, certainly since she'd started school, she could remember feeling that a mistake had been made, that she didn't really belong to her family. "Do you know the story of the ugly duckling?" she asked.

Genia didn't, and Lex told it to her. At the end, she said, "I was the wrong child, not born of my parents—a different species. But with me, it was the reverse of the fairy tale." She sighed, while trying to smile. "I didn't grow up to be a swan. *They* are the swans, all three of them, and I'm the duckling. Or maybe a toad."

All her life, Lex explained, she'd felt the pressure of her parents' social position, the need to be popular, successful, and ambitious and, above all, attractive. Lex was convinced she was none of these, sure she couldn't fulfill her family's expectations. Because they were wonderful—the whole world and Lex herself thought they were wonderful—she found her own existence both painful and embarrassing.

To Genia, Lex had the most one could ask of life. To Lex, Genia's beauty was a quality above all others the world possessed. Though neither could completely understand the other's loneliness, they came together like twin almonds. They formed a shell around themselves; together, they were complete, and even happy.

"That guardian of yours, Merritt—my family knows him, I think. Anyway, I've heard of him before." Lex was sitting cross-legged on her bed. It was a rainy October afternoon, the fourth day since they'd met. "He's a wheeler-dealer."

"What is that?"

"A high-class hustler. Con man. Attractive though, huh?"

"When first I see him, I think he is very handsome. And *kulturny*."

"What's that?"

"Cultured, elegant."

"And now?" Lex brought out a cigarette from under her pillow and lit it. Cigarettes were forbidden everywhere in the school, and most emphatically in the infirmary. She inhaled deeply. "You still think he's neat?"

"I have not spent much time with him. He is—how I say it?—not in the world."

"Out of this world?" Lex tried for meaning. She uncurled her legs, stepped over to Genia's bed, and offered her the cigarette. Genia took a few rapid puffs and returned it. "He is busy. When I arrived on the ship in New York, is too busy to meet me."

"Was," Lex corrected absentmindedly. "How was it on the ship? You have a ball? Say . . ." She held the cigarette between thumb and forefinger, its lighted end toward herself, and examined it. "Maybe we can try a joint one day."

Genia shrugged, not knowing what she meant. Since meeting Lex, Genia had agreed to every scheme or prank. Yesterday they'd pushed each other through the infirmary in a wheelchair until the nurse screamed at them and sent them back to bed. In the evening, Lex ordered pizza from town and, with the lure of a five-dollar tip, persuaded the delivery boy to climb up to the second-floor window to deliver it.

"No ball," Genia said. "Not one dance. I am always with chaperon. Like thing of value somebody might steal. Why would they?"

"You kidding?" Lex asked, taking her last deep drag. "Look at yourself." She ran to flush the butt down the toilet before the nurse came in.

"Well," said the nurse, sniffing suspiciously, "at least I won't have to deal with you hellions much longer. One of you is leaving tomorrow."

"Which one?" Lex asked.

The nurse pointed to Genia. "Her."

"Then we both are," Lex told her as a statement of fact.

The following weekend, Bernard came up to the Ashe-Willmott School for a brief visit. Politely Genia thanked him for the roses he'd sent her in the infirmary.

"I'm glad you liked them." Bernard accepted her gratitude for his thoughtfulness, a memo to his secretary.

They rode out to the Regent's Park Inn, an old and formal New England hotel that served afternoon tea. When they entered the dining room, the guests followed Bernard with their eyes. He was a striking man, Genia knew, very distinguished—and she felt proud to be seen with him.

They were seated beside a window, looking out at the vivid foliage that Genia thought the most beautiful thing in America. Autumn here was like summer in its burst of colors, ranging from yellow to crimson and deep purple. She told Bernard, truthfully, that school was fine. She began telling him about Lex, but on hearing her surname, Bernard pursed his lips. The Vandergrieffs were influential, he admitted, but he'd had unpleasant experiences with some of them. "I don't want you to become friendly with them," he said. Genia was about to protest, when Bernard added quietly, "I brought you something."

His blue eyes were clear as a cold stream below the icy silver of his hair. "Something you've wanted for a long time. A letter from your brother."

She felt giddy again, as with the fever. He brought out the letter. "It's taken two months to reach New York. Here, read it."

She read:

> Leningrad
> 17 August, 1958

My Dear Sister,

You have been much in our thoughts, though we have heard nothing in reply to our letters. May that be a good sign. I'm sure you have many friends by now (perhaps even a boyfriend?) and that you are content.

I am working hard at my studies, and I dare to hope for a place at the university soon. Katya and I are both well, despite my keeping her up until late in the night, with my light on and my pencil scratching away. As I wrote you before, our quarters are quaint as a doll's house.

But never mind, we have our health, and Katya's *piroschki* are as delicious as ever. From our relatives in the country we hear nothing, though there is no reason to doubt that they, too, are healthy and well-fed, on oranges and other good things.

The birthday present I sent you long ago is safe with me here. Never mind, you know that I am thinking of you.

I, too, know you are thinking of me. Therefore, do not waste your time in writing letters. You are always in my heart, as I trust I am in yours.

> Your loving brother,
> Dmitri

Genia finished the letter, dry-eyed and unemotional. "It's not from him," she told Bernard flatly in Russian.

"I'm afraid it is, dear girl."

She shook her head. "He never talked like that. Someone else wrote it. He never called me his 'dear sister.'" Genia,

Genuschka, even Krasavitzsa, her parents' endearment for her, but never "sister."

"The letter had to pass the censor," Bernard explained. "It's a potentially dangerous letter, and he wanted you to beware. It's written in a kind of code, don't you see?"

Genia shook her head. Her hands were beginning to tremble. She pushed away the teacup.

"By addressing you as his 'dear sister' instead of by your name, or whatever pet name the two of you used, he's letting you know that this letter will be read by others, by people who must be assured that everything's clear and aboveboard.

"Now, let's look at it carefully. 'Relatives in the country' means your parents in exile or imprisonment. 'Oranges' probably refers to Siberia, where citrus trees grow. He may or may not have information that your mother or father, or both, are in Siberia. Perhaps he's simply assuming it. As far as my sources can make out, your father is probably within one hundred miles at most from Leningrad."

She stared. "Why don't you know where he is?"

"I'm trying, Genia," he said sharply. "Your mother might be in Siberia, though maybe not. We're working on your father primarily."

She looked at Dmitri's letter again. The handwriting *was* familiar. If the letter was in code, as Bernard said, what did "quaint as a doll's house" mean?

"That they're living in very cramped quarters, I'll bet. Maybe without plumbing. I don't know what they're living on. Could be that your brother has a student's stipend, and the housekeeper has a widow's pension. What's unusual is that they're together."

"His address. What is it?"

"I don't know, Genia. But he's asking you *not* to write to him. The 'birthday present,' whatever it was, was returned. You know that none of his other letters got through to you."

"Why should I not write him?" Her brother, her family.

"Because"—Bernard's voice sounded exasperated—"he asks you not to. His entrance to the university may be jeopardized if you do. Don't forget, here's a boy whose parents have both been sentenced for crimes against society. His sister is probably regarded as a defector."

"Me?" But she didn't need an answer. She hadn't defected any more than her parents had committed crimes. It didn't matter. She folded up the letter and put it in her handbag. Her brother was banished from her again. The letter was a formal announcement that Genia's past was dead.

She closed her handbag and looked at Bernard. What future did he hold out for her? His eyes skimmed over her face. He would be looking at her in just that way, she realized, if she were a photograph or a painting.

Only with Lex, she thought, only with her new friend, did she feel alive, and recognized for who she was. "Please," Genia said, "I want to go back to the school now."

7

Lex arranged to trade rooms with Frankie Rockefeller, who jumped at the chance to be in the senior dorm. To the outside world, Vandergrieff and Rockefeller were practically synonyms, but though Lex and Frankie were vaguely aware that they were classified according to the same rules, and were expected to act like members of the same club, the two girls hadn't exchanged more than "Hello" until the trade took place.

The administration, suffering from the usual difficulty in discriminating between America's two best-known families, didn't discover the switch for two weeks, at which point embarrassment prevented them from taking any more than token action. Lex was settled into the room opposite Genia's, and the girls were inseparable.

They attended different classes, but met immediately afterward. Genia tried out for the swim team, which Lex had belonged to since her first year at Ashe-Willmott, and was immediately accepted. Lex held the school record in the crawl. Genia's summers at the dacha, the daily long swims across the lake, had taught her strength and endurance in the water. After only six weeks on the team, with daily coaching from Lex, Genia was a strong contender for the best free-style-swimmer title.

The girls had all their meals together, did their homework together, washed their hair in adjoining showers, and were

97

separated—except for classes—only when they were asleep. On a Saturday when they were permitted to go into the town, Lex took Genia shopping and, with the allowance money Bernard's lawyers sent Genia regularly on the first and fifteenth of every month, bought her an entire wardrobe at the Nassau Shop: Bermuda shorts, shirts with button-down collars, a few dresses Genia considered "shapeless," but which Lex said were "collegiate," shetland sweaters, and a polo jacket. "You know," Lex said when they'd finished their purchases, "your allowance is about three times what mine is. Just goes to show."

"What?"

"New money comes easier than old. Something like that." She put her arm around Genia's shoulders. "When I was little, I used to think we were poor. I got a quarter a week, and all the other kids got more. But then I learned they were supposed to _save_ their allowance, and I got to spend all of mine. I was a wild spendthrift"—she laughed—"bought up everything in sight: licorice laces, sugar buttons, penny suckers. Candies," she explained.

"I didn't have allowance," Genia said. "Didn't need one. Nothing for me to spend money on."

In her new clothes, her hair held behind her ears with barrettes, Genia felt she was being accepted by the other girls. Her friendship with Lex was respected. Though Lex had a reputation as a "loner," she was not unpopular in school. Having no close friends meant she had no enemies. Belonging to none of the cliques meant she was often asked to mediate disagreements. Her independence and the resonance of her family name made Lex a girl the others looked up to. As her friend, Genia was no longer a strange foreigner or, worse, a suspected Commie.

She and Lex were known, affectionately, as "The Terrible Twos," a label given them by Cynthia Wurlitzer, a senior with an A + in Psychology. Cynthia had found the term in a book on child development by the Gesell Institute, and it perfectly suited the two girls who were forever getting into mischief.

Most of the time, Genia was happy. Weekends sometimes plunged her into a sober thoughtfulness, even melancholy, when she saw the cars drive up to campus, unloading parents who'd come to visit their daughters and take them on an outing or to a restaurant in the town. Nevertheless, by November she felt she belonged at Ashe-Willmott and couldn't remember why she hadn't liked the school when she first arrived. Her cadences when she spoke still marked her as a foreigner, but under Lex's constant tutoring she'd become adept at American slang.

In mid-November they were both sitting cross-legged on the floor in Lex's room, homework spread around them in untidy piles of autumnal paper leaves. The dinner bell sounded from Victoria Woodhull, where their cafeteria was housed. Lex looked up with a sour face, sweeping pages of American Government into Genia's Biology. "Grub again. Want to bet on it? Five to three says sawdust patties smothered in snot."

Genia stretched, smiling broadly. "Seven to four on fish guts with peanut butter."

"You got it." Lex groaned, jumped up, and pulled Genia up from the floor. Walking over the discarded foliage of their homework, they got their jackets and walked out toward "Messy Hall," as Lex called Woodhull.

The trees were bare except for the evergreens, the ground hard and brown. "Look at that," Lex muttered crossly, hands in her pockets. "Turdsville. When is the snow ever going to come? November should be against the law. It doesn't do anybody any good."

"You're right," Genia agreed.

Three girls passed them, scurrying from Susan B. Anthony to dinner. "Hi, TT's!" one of them called out.

Neither Lex nor Genia answered. "Slow," Lex warned. They always tried to be the last ones in, after the other girls were seated, so they could take a table for themselves.

"My last year, and it's got to be November! My last chance for fun before I pass on to the happy hunting grounds."

"Don't know that expression." Genia was walking with the mincing steps of a geisha.

"Death. The place where good girls, girls from good families, like me, stalk their prey. It's called 'coming out,' being a debutante. Dressing up in colored bedsheets and going to dances with a laundry tag dangling from your wrist, and your hair sprayed stiff as cardboard."

"What for?"

"To get married." She wrinkled up her face and aimed her spit at the base of an oak tree. She hit the target. "That's why I won't be going to college next September. A year off for good behavior. That's what they're expecting of me. They figure I might strike it lucky and get someone with breeding—*our kind*, don't you know—to hitch up with me. And if that happens, there'll be no point in me going to college anyway." Though a year and a half older than Genia, Lex had skipped second grade and was young for a high-school senior. Her parents had argued that she should wait until she was eighteen to enter college, and meanwhile she could enjoy her year as a deb.

"Not a chance, though," Lex went on. "Like they say, you can bring the horse to the bar but you can't make it drink whiskey. The deb scene is inhuman. You're supposed to dance with Martians disguised as boys in dinner jackets, who've got nothing but space between the ears and whose only topic of conversation is themselves."

Genia was laughing. "Don't go to the dances," she suggested.

"Are you *serious*? That's like telling me not to go to my own funeral. I mean, it would kill my parents. But," Lex said in a subdued voice, "it kills me. It really does. I mean, *look* at me."

Genia turned. In the outer circumference of Messy Hall's floodlights she saw a chunky girl with medium-brown hair, small features, wide mouth, and determined chin, her face now contorted into a grimace.

"I am *not* your deb of the year," she said bitterly. "Not your ordinary, run-of-the-mill, plain-Jane deb either. I'm a rat. If anyone talks to me at those dances, it'll only be to keep me distracted so I won't bite. I'm ugly, and I'm mean. I can't say the things you're supposed to say to the Martians: 'Oooh, what a perfectly gorgeous tie! Where on earth did you find it? In a store? How perfectly magnificent! How very-very clever of you!'" Lex stopped her mimicry for a moment to let Genia catch her breath from laughter. Then she went on: "Or it's 'What splendid things you have on your arm! They're muscles? I thought they were the Himalayas.' Morons, creeps. You're not supposed to curse in front of them or smoke a cigarette or cross your legs, or even breathe as far as I know. It 'threatens' them. They've all got this cute little thing called 'the male ego' and it crumbles apart the moment a girl says 'shit.' I'm serious, it's a funny farm out there."

Genia hugged her. "*You* are funny. I bet boys love you."

"Fuck them," Lex said bitterly.

Genia had never heard her use that word before. She stepped back, but Lex reached out for her hand. "You. You're the one who's lovable. I was nothing till you came here, I mean it. Just an ugly mug. And look at you. Beautiful, the most beautiful goddamn girl in the world. If you were in my shoes, you'd be deb of the century."

They walked into the cafeteria and sat down at an empty table. No one looked up; they were used to the late arrivals of the Terrible Twos.

"You had to wait until my last year to show up," Lex went on. "I feel more alive than I ever have."

"Me too!" Genia exclaimed.

The server gave them an angry glance and banged their plates down in front of them.

"You're magic: Genia the magician," Lex said, squeezing her hand. "No, Genia the genie. That's it!"

Lex sprang up and tapped her knife loudly against her water glass until the room became silent. "Attention!" she announced. "We are about to have a christening!"

Some of the girls began giggling, unsure what the Twos were up to now. Lex held her glass above Genia, and with her right hand lavishly doused Genia's hair. "I anoint you Genie, performer of miracles!"

There was loud laughter as Lex sat down. "Is it okay?" she whispered nervously to her friend.

"I like it very much," said the new Genie, smiling as she shook the water from her hair.

Lex didn't return to the subject of her deadly future again. Instead, she issued a rallying cry to Genie: "Stamp out November! Bring on the Revolution!"

"They used to talk so at home," said Genie, laughing. It relieved her to make jokes about Russia.

"Yeah, but *they* carried it to extremes. I'm just thinking about a little excitement."

Genie continued to give in to Lex's schemes. They wrote a love letter to Miss Thrasher, the chemistry teacher, and signed it with the name of the French teacher, Pierre Rousseau. Then they wrote to Monsieur Rousseau inviting him for a candlelight supper and signed it "Mary Thrasher." They watched the two teachers carefully, sure they were detecting signs of incipient romance. But all was still and no scandal ensued.

They went on to liquor, spiking a watermelon with a bottle of vodka and selling slices of it to girls in the dorm.

On Wednesday evening, the housemother noticed a few girls weaving through the Susan B. Anthony house, and next day Lex and Genie were given a harsh reprimand by Miss Willmott in her office. The headmistress (granddaughter of the founder) informed them that the Ashe-Willmott School was not a place for "hooligans and alcoholics."

They giggled, but they curtailed their pranks for a while. Not until the February blacks (worse than the November blues) hit them did the girls embark on a new escapade. When they did, it was a sensation.

Lex was the mastermind, Genie the technician. She studied her chemistry books, slipped into the lab some evenings to try out different formulae, and after two weeks came up with what they were looking for. She brought the colorless liquid to Lex in triumph: "The secret of womanhood!"

On the eve before the swim meet with Ashe-Willmott's archrival from Greenwich, the girls made their way to the pool and dropped a container into the water.

Next day at ten, the meet began. Greenwich won the crawl and backstroke. Ashe-Willmott took the free style and breast-stroke. Halfway into the marathon, Greenwich was in the lead.

Sitting at the edge of the pool, Lex dangled her hand in the water and released the chemical reagent from its small plastic container.

As the water turned blood red around Greenwich's lead swimmer, she faltered and then floundered in embarrassment. The redness spread through the pool and the marathon was thrown into confusion. The event was declared a forfeit.

"A miscarriage would be better," Lex whispered to Genie.

The laughter of the two girls was not lost on the swim coach, who reported his suspicions to Miss Willmott. The head-mistress called the girls into her office and interrogated them so closely that they were forced to confess. She put them both on suspension.

Next day Lex's parents arrived at the school and Genie met them for a brief moment in Lex's room before they went to see Miss Willmott. Margaret Vandergrieff was exceptionally tall, with a thin, square body that resembled a plinth of wood. Phillip, Lex's father, was smaller and rounder than his wife. His nearly lashless eyes peered through his glasses with a look of curiosity and intelligence. Lex was subdued with them, almost sullen.

Bernard Merritt didn't come to the school, though Genie learned later in the day that he'd spoken to Miss Willmott by phone. If she'd been his own child, Genie wondered, would he have come? Phillip Vandergrieff was surely a very busy man, yet he'd put his daughter ahead of all his business.

Would her own parents have come here to protect her? Or would they have been ashamed of her? She couldn't imagine either of them arriving at Ashe-Willmott to speak to the headmistress. She couldn't imagine them speaking English, or picture them in America. Her parents, though not dead, were buried.

Genie received a letter from Bernard, warning her against trying such a "damn-fool" thing again. He reminded her that she was a guest in America, and must behave accordingly.

That sentence chilled her. "Guest" meant she wasn't to consider herself at home even in her school. His next sentence was a reminder that the Vandergrieff girl was not the right companion for her.

A cold, terrible letter. He didn't seem to care about her at all. Why had he brought her to America?

Because he'd promised her father; only for that reason. Her father was in prison, and Dmitri, too, was locked away from her. She had only Bernard to turn to, and he seemed more a warden than a guardian.

The Vandergrieffs' immediate visit, and particularly the presence of Phillip Vandergrieff in her office, influenced Miss Willmott to change her mind. The girls were reinstated after Easter and remained paragons of behavior until the end of the school year.

"We'll be able to go wild over the summer," Lex reassured Genie, as well as herself. They planned to spend it together, at the Vandergrieffs' estate in the Adirondacks. Lex painted a picture of paradise, or something very close to it, where they would be free to roam through the mountains and forests, swim and boat in the lake, ride horses, go water-skiing, picnic in secret clearings, with no one to supervise or reprimand. A natural paradise for the two of them, with no Miss Willmott lurking behind a tree.

But two weeks before Lex's graduation, the dream was

shattered. Genie had put off telling Bernard her plans until late May. Then she wrote to him, and he phoned the dorm as soon as he read her letter, leaving an angry message to have Genie call him back immediately.

She knew it was off before he told her, and she had thoughts of running away, hiding out at the Vandergrieffs', never returning.

"You're my responsibility," Bernard was saying, "for as long as you're in this country. I brought you here, I'm responsible for you, and you'll do what I say."

"But they have invited me—you can ask her parents," she pleaded, knowing it was useless.

"I'm not going to talk to anyone's parents! You seem to have a mistaken idea of who's who. You take your orders from *me*, not the other way around. I've arranged for you to spend the summer on Cape Cod. You'll be a mother's helper, or whatever the hell they call it. You'll be taking care of the child of one of my company executives. A perfect job for you, in a beautiful part of the country."

"Please. Don't make me go."

The naked loneliness in her voice softened him for only a moment. "I don't believe I'm being unfair, Genia. Most American teenagers work in the summer. I certainly did, at your age. Worked my balls off. That's why I'm where I am today. Doing nothing, having fun—that's for little kids and bums. And you're neither, Genia. Everything's been put in your lap so far. Now you've got to learn to get up and start moving on your own."

She hung up, too depressed to tell Lex about the phone call for several hours. Bernard was terribly unfair—how could he say that everything had been given to her? It was the other way around—everything had been taken away. Through Lex, she'd had a chance to put things together. . . .

Lex found her at four in the afternoon, lying on the bed, tears trickling down the sides of her face into her hair. "I waited for you after your class. What's wrong?"

Genie told her. Lex sat down on the bed, and the girls regarded each other in silence. Then Genie sat up. "I'll finish school," she said with resolution. "Then I will go away somewhere and not see him again."

"Sure," said Lex.

"I'll get a job, become a doctor—"

"Hold on. You're not making sense, you know."

"I know," she said.

"The guy's a bastard. An out-and-out shit. And he's got you in the palm of his hand. This summer will be hell, black sulfurous hell. Then you'll come back here to Ashes-and-Dust and I'll be dead on the happy hunting grounds."

They were silent again, contemplating the bleakness of their lives ahead.

Lex saw a faint light. "It'll be Christmas, and you'll come stay with us—if we're both still around by then. I'll make my father get on Bernard's ass. He'll do it for me. And my father has a way of making things happen. You'll see. Christmas."

But to both of them it sounded like the next millennium. "Maybe," Genie said, "Bernard is trying to do the best for me."

"If that were true, we'd be spending the summer together."

"No. I mean, it's true I am not independent. Maybe he wants me to learn that. Maybe he is trying to be as my father."

"He's not your father."

Genie nodded, as the tears started again.

Three weeks later, Genie was in Truro, a township on Cape Cod's National Seashore bordering Provincetown at the last lick of the Cape, where the land curls in on itself like a tongue reaching back.

The house was in the backwoods, reached by a narrow sand road that wandered off from Route 6 and wound through woods and swamps, forking and branching like arteries to the hidden summer houses of Bostonians and New Yorkers, mainly New Yorkers. The Thompsons had been renting the same house for ten summers, each year intending to build one of their own. But since the birth of their daughter, Cindy, five years earlier, they'd become uncertain about what type of place to build. Whenever they spoke of looking around for land, they'd remind each other, "Let's wait until Cindy's, well, um, *seen* to." By that they meant until Cindy was put away in a home for the retarded. Even with their means—moderately substantial—the Thompsons couldn't afford the cost of keeping Cindy in a private establishment for the rest of her natural life. They waited, hoping that as she grew older, perhaps when she came to school age, she would be diagnosed as permanently and severely handicapped, permitting the Thompsons to receive financial aid when they put her away.

Genie traveled up to her summer job by bus, changing at Providence, Rhode Island, and again at Hyannis on the Cape. When she arrived in Truro, Mrs. Thompson met her in a Land Rover, a car with four-wheel drive that became nearly the sole topic of her conversation all the way home. As they pulled into the driveway, Naomi Thompson told Genie that her job would be easy—all she had to do was make sure the child was fed and kept out of danger.

When they entered the house, Mrs. Thompson pointed in the direction of a closed door. "Go in and meet Cindy. Your room is right next to hers."

Genie opened the door with trepidation. The child was sitting in a corner on the floor. The room was nearly bare, a colored beach ball the only toy.

"Hello," Genie said nervously.

The child didn't answer. She was thin, pale, and looked undernourished. Her face was bizarre, though in the first moment Genie couldn't place what was wrong with it.

"Hello, Cindy"—again, but the child gave no sign of having heard. The head was malformed, Genie realized, the girl had no cheekbones. Her face resembled a rodent's.

Cindy had been born with Treacher-Collins syndrome, her mother said when Genie came out of the room. A congenital malformation of the skull. "Everyone in my family is normal"—Naomi Thompson seemed to be acquitting herself— "and in Matt's too. We don't know how it happened.

"You'll be free a lot of the time," the child's mother went on. "You don't have to do much with her. She doesn't understand things."

But in the next days, Genie learned that wasn't true. Cindy wasn't retarded or dumb, she was simply very frightened. And extremely sensitive, responding to a harsh tone of voice or a look of displeasure by curling herself into a ball. She stiffened at unaccustomed noise, remained frozen if she sensed danger. When Genie reached out her hand, Cindy shrank back as though afraid it would strike her.

Her parents treated their child like a pet that had outlived its ability to please, avoiding her whenever possible. Genie was alone with Cindy most of the time. Her father, Matt Thompson, stayed in New York during the week, usually flying up on Friday nights to the tiny Provincetown airport, where Naomi would drive to meet him. Weekends were spent in what Naomi called "wall-to-wall" tennis, and evenings they went to gallery openings, cocktail parties, and dinners out. During the week, Naomi was very busy as a "grass widow" (Genie didn't understand that expression either), in early-morning tennis, breakfast with a friend, then hours at the beach, tanning and playing in the waves. Afterward she "washed off" in a pond, usually swimming its entire length, before returning home to do her hair and prepare for her evening out.

Naomi dropped Genie and Cindy at the beach every day, telling them to "have fun." She'd given Genie a waterproof wristwatch—a crude, almost caricature version of the one Bernard had given her father—so that Genie would be back at the parking lot at the appointed time.

Genie always walked Cindy the same way down the beach, away from the people and ball playing, close to the dunes (Cindy was afraid of the pounding waves), until they were equidistant between the town beaches of Truro and its western neighbor, Wellfleet. Alone, as far as they could see in either direction, they found a place in the dunes to sit and have the picnic lunch Genie had made for them earlier in the morning.

As time passed, Cindy began to trust Genie. She took Genie's hand as they walked, holding on with both of her own. Each day they inched nearer the water, until Cindy was able to walk on the wet sand. Next day she was confident enough to sit on it, and watch as Genie made a sand fort.

Her first words to Genie were soft but clearly enunciated: "Want to be a mouse."

"Why a mouse?" Genie tried not to appear startled.

"In a mousehole," Cindy explained.

Genie understood. "When I was little girl," she told Cindy, "I lived in beautiful country, full of snow. My daddy was a snowman. Nobody liked to look at him."

The child's face was full of interest. "But was my daddy," Genie went on, "and I loved him."

"Yes," said Cindy. Every day after that, she begged Genie to, "Tell me snowman."

Every day Genie thought up little stories about her father. Sometimes she invented them. It didn't matter. Cindy loved "Snowman."

Genie wrote to Lex every day, as though keeping a journal. She still wrote English better than she spoke. She was adept at both, but occasionally in speaking she still dropped pronouns or used the present tense for the past. "Cindy's mother told me that surgery wouldn't do any good. A waste of money. And when I asked Mr. Thompson, he looked at me as if I should be minding my own business and he said, 'She's too young.'

"They don't realize that their child is a human being, Lex. Cindy gave me five pebbles today. She placed them in a ring.

"She has feelings. She's a person. But her parents don't see that. Or they pretend they don't—or maybe they just don't want to."

Genie despised the Thompsons so much she found it difficult to be in the same room with them. But she felt she was a buffer between them and their child. She'd learned from Mrs. Thompson that in their New York apartment Cindy was left in the care of a maid who seemed to have no interest in children, particularly not "handicapped" ones. When the end of summer approached, Genie dreaded the effect her leaving would have on Cindy.

"You know, Lex, it's crazy. Like throwing away a diamond because you don't like what it's wrapped in. Cindy taught me more than I taught her this summer. She made me see that my father was living in a mousehole all my life, except it was called his study. I don't know if that's what he wanted, or if he was forced to stay there and not come out because of his face.

"Maybe it's the same thing. If other people are frightened by the way you look, or disgusted, then you learn to be frightened or disgusted at yourself. It isn't fair. Why shouldn't everybody look normal?"

Genie stayed on till the end of August. The Thompsons commended her for her patience and offered her a bonus. She refused, and the anger coiled inside her was ready to strike, but in that moment Cindy shuffled in, and Genie controlled her anger for the child's sake.

When Cindy saw the packed suitcase next to Genie she began to howl. Then she screamed, with the same high, terrified sounds she made when thunder crashed.

"Cindy . . . Cindy . . ." Genie was crouched down beside the child, her arms open to embrace her. For a moment, Cindy stopped her screaming. She looked at Genie with clear understanding of what was about to happen. "Bad snowman," she said, and then she started again.

Genie could hear her screams as she walked out of the house, even when she was inside the car as it backed out the driveway.

* * *

"I've *got* to become a doctor," Genie wrote to Lex. "I've got to change people's faces."

The answering letter arrived for Genie at Ashe-Willmott. "How about changing *my* face," it began, "into one just like yours?"

Genie smiled; a typical Lex remark. To Genie, Lex looked just right, the way she should look—like Lex.

But she couldn't put Cindy's little face and her huge terror out of her mind. As the semester began, Genie developed a consuming interest in plastic surgery. She read what she could about it in magazines, and longed to go deeper into the subject, to find the books that would teach her what she felt she had to know.

Over the summer, she'd seen that disfigurement warped the soul along with the body. Unless Cindy's face could be changed, she'd never become normal. Giorgi had been disfigured as an adult, after his personality had developed, but still, Genie was sure, the disfigurement had changed him, transformed him from the outside in. He might not be banished now, nor she in America, if his face looked like that of any other man.

She was determined to learn more about plastic surgery. Now that she was a senior, and had the academic standard required for permission to work on a special project, she proposed her topic to her social-studies teacher. But he was skeptical. "Plastic surgery," he said, "is frivolous. Not a valid subject for an Ashe-Willmott girl."

"No," Genie argued. "Is for people who are deformed."

"Face lifts," the teacher went on. "Changing the shape of noses. Aging movie stars who don't want to look their age. If you're interested in medicine, study something of more general value—healing, the cure of diseases—"

"Please," she interrupted. "Let me tell you." He listened while she talked about her summer with Cindy. Genie became impassioned as she described the way Cindy was treated by her parents. At the end, he relented. She could do a special report on plastic surgery, but only on condition that she limit her report to its history. "You'll find out about the latest methods when you're older," he said, "if you ever do study medicine. We like our girls to build a foundation here for future study. Learn about the past of the subject—if there is one."

Genie received permission to go to New York for research at the library of the New York Academy of Medicine, which was open to the public. On each of her three trips to the city—two hours by train—Genie stayed overnight at Bernard's apartment.

He was in town on only one of those nights, in early November, but had a dinner engagement with the French ambassador. When he came home to change into formal clothes, Bernard spent a few minutes talking with Genie. He told her that the news from Russia hadn't changed in the past seven weeks, when he'd learned that Giorgi was undergoing "reeducation" in a special "training camp" not far from Gorky. Dmitri was enrolled at the university. Natasha's whereabouts were not known—though, Bernard admitted, he hadn't placed the same priority on her as on her husband.

"Things are going well at school, Genia?"

"I'm Genie now," she said. They were in his dressing room, where Gregori had just made a perfect bow tie and was holding out the dinner jacket. They spoke English to each other. "Genia" belonged to their Russian time.

"Genie?"

"I told you before," she reminded him.

Bernard inspected himself briefly in the mirror and gave a nod of satisfaction. "Must've slipped my mind. I'll always see you as Genia, the little girl with the bashful eyes and a fall of titian hair. You should let it grow, I think. This style doesn't suit you."

"It's what everyone wears."

"All the more reason for you not to. Are you receiving your allowance? Good. Is it adequate for your needs?"

She nodded. "It's more than I need."

Bernard smiled, pleased at the acknowledgment of his generosity. "You'll be getting a bonus around Christmastime. I'll have to be abroad then, I'm afraid. Mainly business, though I'm planning a little stopover in St. Moritz. But I want you to enjoy yourself, so I've arranged for you to have extra spending money."

The word "bonus" aroused her indignation. She was not a "thing" to be bought, not by the Thompsons and not by him. But the thought of Bernard being away over Christmas also made her feel lonely. She'd learned that Christmas was for families. "Thank you," she said politely.

He kissed her high on the forehead, at the hairline. "I won't wake you when I leave tomorrow. Have a good dinner with Sonya. I'll talk to you Sunday."

He strode out, looking grand and distinguished in his evening dress. Like a monarch, she thought, remote and powerful, who would never do more than confer favors on her: his subject, not his daughter.

She was fifteen, a senior at school, expected to act mature. But why didn't he take her with him? Why didn't he ever speak to her about his business, about his life? At least he could take her into his confidence; she would understand. But he didn't treat her as an adult—or as his child either.

When Bernard was away, Genie spent her time in the kitchen with Sonya, who always brought out a profusion of delicacies that overwhelmed even Genie's school-starved appetite. She'd stuff herself to give Sonya pleasure, eating beyond satiation. Sonya was Genie's haven, a motherly, loving woman. Genie liked Gregori too, but he was patriarchal and sometimes intimidating.

The Leontovs were White Russians who had fled from home before the Revolution of 1917. Nineteen-year-old Gregori had run by himself from Moscow, from the oncoming tide of Bolshevism. Sonya, then eleven, had left with her parents from St. Petersburg, which had recently been renamed Petrograd.

They met in Paris two years later and Sonya fell in love at her first sight of Gregori's blue eyes and blond mustache. She married him as soon as she turned sixteen. After two years of marriage, they learned that Sonya was barren. They grieved together for five years, while working as a couple in fashionable homes and small restaurants. Then, resigned to being childless, they decided to open a restaurant, and decorated it in the style of their parents' homes in Russia. They served the food of their childhood to émigrés like themselves, who congregated there regularly, singing and reminiscing but often unable to cover the price of the dinner.

The Leontovs extended credit until they themselves were hounded by creditors. Unable to collect on debts owing to them, regarded by banks as a poor risk for a loan, the Leontovs ended in bankruptcy. They applied for the positions of cook and waiter in a neighborhood bistro.

When Bernard met them, they were working at the prestigious Lapérouse, a restaurant on the quai, where Sonya was chef of hors d'oeuvres. Bernard tasted the tiny mouth-watering *blinis* and demanded to meet their maker.

The war had just begun, and Bernard was one of the only foreigners dining in the restaurant. The future of service establishments in Paris looked dim. When Bernard offered to hire Sonya and Gregori, they accepted immediately. He would arrange for their visas and pay their passage. Their gratitude was exorbitant, and Bernard was delighted both by his magnanimity and by his discovery of a domestic couple that seemed custom-made for him. Native Russian speakers in his household would ensure his continued fluency in the language.

But despite his urgings of the State Department, visas were not issued for the Leontovs until 1941. They arrived in New York on the day the Nazis invaded France, and the coincidence confirmed to them that Bernard Merritt had saved their lives.

In Genie they saw another refugee saved from death by their benefactor. Because of her age, she seemed a daughter to them, though, as Bernard Merritt's ward, she belonged to a higher class. Gregori expressed his pleasure at Genie's visits by smiling frequently. Sonya arranged fresh flowers in her room, brought her breakfast in bed, and prepared her bath with scented oils.

Genie loved sitting in the kitchen as Sonya told stories of old Russia, of her childhood and the days of her parents' and grandparents' childhoods. She was as inventive in storytelling as in cooking. With each recounting, the relatives became more eccentric and delightful. Uncle Vladimir ran off with a circus acrobat, who became in the next telling a tightrope walker, then a lion tamer. Great-Aunt Anja built a Turkish mosque in her enormous garden and kept a young Turkish poet there, to produce rhymes for family occasions. Great-Uncle Ivan was a cossack who played chess in his head, winning each game from his friend as they rode their horses over the steppes.

Sonya's deep voice embroidered the stories until they were rich tapestries of a mythical past they both shared. Genie was enraptured, but on her research trips to New York she forced herself to break away from the spell to work in her sitting room. Sonya would encourage her to go up, and a few hours later knocked softly at her door, bringing in a silver tray with

two glasses of tea. When Genie took the train back to school,
Sonya accompanied her in the car to the railroad station.

Genie was trying to complete her paper before Christmas,
to leave her free over the vacation. Bernard hadn't approved
her proposed visit to the Vandergrieffs when she first mentioned it, but eventually he gave in, though not graciously.
Genie wondered if Phillip Vandergrieff had indeed "gotten on
Bernard's ass." She didn't know what that could mean, but
Lex's phrase was so peculiar that Genie had remembered it.

She did nothing but work, sleep, and eat during the weeks
preceding Christmas. The topic of her special report was
interesting, though she would have preferred to write on
something with closer bearing on Cindy or her father.

Plastic surgery, she learned, began in ancient India, where
noses were sliced off as punishment for crimes (including
adultery) and in war. In the seventh century B.C. a surgeon
named Sushruta described the procedure for reconstructing
amputated noses, explained how to perform skin transplants,
and gave descriptions of surgical instruments.

Sushruta's writings were not translated into Latin until the
nineteenth century, when an English surgeon performed two
successful operations by the "Indian" method, using a plate of
wax, molded into the shape of the nose, then placed on the
patient's forehead and flattened. The surgeon drew a line
around the wax, removed it, and dissected the skin along the
outline, leaving uncut a slip between the eyes. The flap was
brought down, reversed to bring the skin side up, and sutured
to its new position, creating a nose.

Genie drew a series of sketches to illustrate the procedure.
Then she continued to the "Italian" method, developed in the
1400's by Branca, a Sicilian surgeon. A century later, Gasparo
Tagliacozzi, professor of anatomy and medicine at Bologna,
wrote a book detailing all known surgical reconstructions of
mutilated parts of the body. He later became known as "the
father of plastic surgery."

Genie headed her Italian section with a quote from Tagliacozzi: "We restore, repair, and make whole parts which nature
hath given, but which *fortune* hath taken away."

She copied out the sentence again, in her best script, and
pinned it to her wall. It was beautifully put, she thought: the
noble purpose of plastic surgeons.

"Fortune" in the twentieth century applied mainly to wars. In World War I a band of medical men and women from Harvard went to the aid of the British Army in France. V. H. Kasanjian, "the miracle man of the Western Front," as King George V referred to him, reconstructed shattered and missing jaws on the battlefield, and became the founder of modern plastic surgery.

Each succeeding war brought a greater array and number of casualties. Advanced technology meant new kinds of weapons and new types of injuries they could inflict. It also meant improved transportation. Soldiers who would have died in an earlier war through loss of blood survived their smashed jaws, hands, or blown-away faces. These survivors could be operated on after the life-threatening emergency was over, and reconstructive surgery could be performed in stages, sometimes over a number of years.

Genie received an A− on her paper, not an A, because instead of a general conclusion, Genie summed up her report in a sentence the social-studies teacher labeled a non-sequitur: "There were 250,000 cases of frostbite in World War II."

8

The small jet dipped over the wooded mountains, powdered lightly with snow as though gauze had been placed over the evergreens. In her leather lounging chair, Genie was the only guest among the passengers of the private plane. The others were coming to work at the Vandergrieffs' Topnotch over the vacation period, when the regular skeleton staff couldn't handle the additional demands of the family and their guests.

Genie picked up the ringing wall phone to her right. "It's me." Lex's voice was clear. "I can see you with my binoculars. I can't wait!"

"Want me to parachute down now?"

"No," Lex said, laughing. "I'd never find you in the woods. It's been so long!"

A few minutes later, Genie could make out a stick figure jumping up and down and throwing her arms so wide it seemed she was expecting the plane to fly into them.

Though Lex had often talked about Topnotch, it wasn't at all what Genie expected. From the air, at least, it appeared to be a wilderness camp, with log cabins built in a semicircle around the largest of them, the "manor," she supposed, that looked as though it were made up of three or four cabins. The houses blended with the woods, and the woods seemed to go on for miles, interrupted only by a large pale gray circle. That was the lake Lex had told her about, set among the trees like a mirror to reflect the sky.

The plane descended, barely skirting the treetops, and Genie lost sight of the strip where Lex had been gesticulating. The wheels touched ground with a dull thud and rolled along a narrow runway invisible from the air. The plane turned, taxied back on a parallel runway, and came to a halt beside the radar tower. When the engine stopped, Lex yanked open the door and ran into the cabin just as Genie was getting out of her chair.

No bear could hug so fiercely, Genie thought. She hugged her back with bone-crushing affection, and when Lex led them down from the plane, both girls were panting.

"I thought you'd never get here. I thought Bernard would screw it up somehow."

"He's traveling, won't be home for the whole vacation. But he let me come. What did your father say to him?"

"I'm not sure, but Uncle Judson—Dad's brother—heads the board of an oil conglomerate, and Bernard's involved in oil too, so I guess Dad reminded him that it's good business to remain friendly. Something like that." Lex's breath steamed in the cold air as she spoke.

Genie giggled. "You look like someone in a cartoon. Your words come out of your mouth in white balloons." She stopped and hugged herself. "Is this really Topnotch? Am I really here?"

Lex pinched Genie's cheek, already rosy in the cold. "Offhand, I'd say yes—but that's just an uninformed opinion."

"Oh, Lex"—Genie touched her arm—"I *did* miss you."

"That's less than half of it," Lex answered, taking Genie's mittened hand in her gloved one. "They'll bring your bags. Want to run? You look cold."

"I am," Genie admitted. The fur jacket Bernard had given her two years earlier was much too small. The sleeves were short, and it fitted too tightly around her chest, permitting no cushion of warmed air next to her body. She had a warm down jacket in her luggage, but Genie had thought fur would be more appropriate for her first arrival at the Vandergrieffs'.

Holding hands, they ran to the main house and came into a large room with a blazing fire in the massive fireplace, sending out an evocative woodsy smell. Despite its size, the room seemed cozy. The couch was strewn with hand-embroidered pillows, a bear rug lay on the floor, snowshoes hung from a hook on the wall. She thought of Finland, the Krukkalas' house. This house, too, was rustic and northern—not at all what she'd imagined when she'd dressed in her fur.

She felt conspicuous as Margaret Vandergrieff came up to her wearing plaid wool slacks and a navy sweatshirt. Genie had imagined a place like Bernard's, filled with art objects and delicate furniture.

"So glad you could make it!" said Lex's mother, giving Genie a powerful handshake. "I've been hearing nothing but 'Genie this' and 'Genie that' since Lex has been home, and I was beginning to wonder if you might not be a genie of her imagination."

"We met before," Genie said, smiling. "Up at school."

"Don't remind me! That was in your juvenile-delinquent days. You look frozen, poor dear. Come close to the fire. How about a cup of hot chocolate? Tea?"

"Tea, please. Thank you."

"Good. I'll tell Mary. Make yourself at home. Lex will take you to your house in a moment, after you've warmed up."

Genie turned to Lex in surprise as her mother walked out to order the tea. "*My* house?"

"Yours and mine. I told Mom we wanted one of the cabins to ourselves so we could have some privacy. Not be around *them* all the time."

"Fabulous." A little house of their own in the snowy woods, where they could do what they liked and talk all night long! Genie was exhilarated at the thought of so much freedom, such happiness.

Lex's mother brought in the tea herself on a wooden tray. "Call me Meg," she said, "it's easiest. We're informal around here, you'll see. The only rules we have are No Smoking in the Woods and Dinner at Seven, though sometimes we miss by a wide margin. Whatever you need, please let me know about it. We have skis for you—you'll have to look through the boots, though, to see which of them fit, and then we'll adjust the bindings. Though right now there's not enough snow on the ground to cover the bald spots."

The three of them sat on the floor in front of the fire, their teacups on a low table, and Genie was fascinated by Meg's rapid-fire talk, warm and easy, as though they were old friends. Genie could see a lot of Lex in her, the bustling energy, the hint of adventure in the way she talked, with a slight breathlessness at the end of each sentence. But Meg was half a foot taller than Lex, very lean—and Lex was definitely overweight—with paler hair and skin and a large, well-formed nose. Physically, they would never be taken for mother and daughter, but their animation was the same, and Genie felt the kind of immediate attraction to Meg she had on meeting Lex.

When they were nearly finished with their tea, Phillip Vandergrieff came in, demanding in a stern voice, "Where is the genie?"

Genie stood up and shook hands. She recognized Lex's father easily from the brief moment when she'd met him. The round face and nearly lashless eyes behind horn-rimmed glasses looked at her kindly but appraisingly, somewhat as Bernard had first looked at her. "So. We meet again, young ruffian." He smiled. "My daughter's fellow conspirator. I don't doubt that you will come up with all sorts of terrible schemes in your cabin, but luckily the pool is closed and we have no chemistry lab on the premises."

"Daddy!" Lex rebuked him, while Genie smiled uncertainly, not sure if his teasing was meant affectionately or as a reproach.

"Conspiracy is good training," he went on, with a wink at Lex, who frowned and looked away. "It's the basis of business, government, the arts and sciences, religion—all human endeavor is, at base, a conspiracy."

"Oh, Phillip," Meg said with a light laugh, "let Genie unpack before you start converting her." To Genie she said, "Phillip is an apostle, you know. Maybe Lex has told you, her father lost his calling as a preacher."

"Me?" Phillip asked with an innocent smile. "A preacher? I have preached to no one but my dog, and she, I'm sorry to say, fell asleep at the beginning of the sermon."

Meg laughed, Lex gave a faint smile, and whatever slight rift there had been was smoothed over. "Come on," Lex said to Genie. "It's time to inspect our home."

Their cabin was approximately seventy-five yards from the main building, and though smaller, had the same atmosphere of rustic coziness. Downstairs was a living/dining room and kitchen, upstairs two bedrooms, each with bathroom. All rooms, except for the bathrooms, had fireplaces, and the little house was a perfect blend of comfort and simplicity. The bedrooms were sparsely furnished under the slope of the roof, but the beds were large, on brass bedstands, with fluffy down comforters. Everything in the house was functional, the only adornments being old family photographs and a sampler on the walls of the downstairs room.

"It's perfect," said Genie. "You don't know how lucky you are."

Lex wrinkled up her face and sat down on Genie's bed while Genie unpacked. "Your mother's like you—straightforward. She's charming."

Lex nodded. "She knows how to put it on."

"What do you mean?"

"Nothing. She's charming, as you said, and everybody's crazy about her. She's the real dynamo behind everything, runs the houses, takes care of the property, hires and fires, makes most of the decisions."

"But your father . . ." Genie was putting her clothes in the plain wooden wardrobe.

"I'm coming to him. Anyway, Mom makes the decisions—but they're never important ones. She'll decide what bushes or flowers to plant, what's for dinner, if it's time to hire an extra cook. That sort of thing. Day-by-day life, I guess. Meanwhile, Dad's running the Vandergrieff Foundation, scientific research, social welfare, special projects of all kinds. Does other things too, but the Foundation's really his baby. *His* decisions affect the world, and hers . . . well, it's the old man-woman thing. Any decision Mom makes can't be important, for the simple reason that it's made by a woman."

"I don't understand," Genie said, sliding her suitcase under the bed.

"Mom was poor when she married Dad. Not dirt-poor, her father was a high-school principal. But there were other kids in the family, her mom didn't work, and there wasn't any extra money. Marrying a Vandergrieff was the most important thing that happened in her life, and it's her career. It's what she *does*, Genie, her life's work is being Mrs. Phillip Vandergrieff. Charm goes with the job. It's part of her business to make everybody like her—any one of those people might be of use to her husband one day."

"You're terribly cynical." Genie was shocked. "That's a mean way to talk."

"I guess. Let's drop it." Lex reached out suddenly for Genie's hand. "Maybe I *am* mean, but it's just that . . . well, everything's so *easy* for all of them. They've got thousands of friends, they're invited to so many parties and things that they can't go to even a tenth of them, and I feel invisible, or else in their way—the ugly, uncharming offspring nobody wants to know about." She looked up at Genie, and the pain on her face was unmistakable. "Please, stay *my* friend. Always."

Genie squeezed her hand. "You're like my sister."

"Sister," Lex repeated. She shook her head briskly and stood up. "Let's go down and light a fire, get a couple of beers, and you tell me all the gossip about old Ashes-and-Dust."

Christmas was planned as a family affair. That meant Lex's brother Pel, their grandmother (Meg's mother), and their Uncle Henry, Phillip's younger brother, now governor of New Jersey, who would be flying up with his family and sister-in-law.

On the twenty-third of December, Pel arrived at Topnotch with his grandmother. Rose Borden was as angular as her daughter, and a nonstop talker. Widowed for the past five years, she was still unaccustomed to living alone, and she compensated for her solitude by intense sociability whenever she was among people. She missed having someone to fuss over, and her tall, brilliant grandson was her first choice. She was clinging to his arm when Genie met them that evening.

Pel towered over her, over his mother too, despite her nearly six feet of height. He was as thin as she was, his body stretched like taffy, and his limbs seemed attached to his long trunk as an afterthought.

Even as he came forward to meet Genie, he stumbled, but righted himself immediately. "So it's you at last. A pleasure to meet you."

"You too," Genie mumbled. The way he was looking at her made her aware that her flannel shirt was open one button more than it should have been. Her hand instinctively flew up to cover the cleft.

Pel was still smiling at her. "When I heard you were from Russia, I pictured you on a tractor. I didn't know Soviet girls could be so feminine. Despite what we've been led to believe, the Soviets *must* be ahead of us." Genie knew he was a graduate student at the Woodrow Wilson School of International Affairs at Princeton. He was twenty-two years old, and yet he seemed to be flirting with her!

"Americans," she answered brazenly, looking up at his height, "will touch the moon first, just by reaching up."

She was glad of his answering laughter. Genie decided he

sounded like Lex when he talked, his words rushing together and spilling out as if he had no way of controlling them.

"What a pretty girl," said Rose Borden, frowning at her grandson. "How do you like America?"

"Medium-rare," answered Genie. Lex gave a hoot of laughter behind her, and Pel grinned, nodding his head. But, seeing the bewilderment on the old lady's face, Genie quickly added, "Very much, I think America is wonderful."

"We welcome people from every land," Rose Borden informed her sternly, "to share in the American dream, which means opportunity for all, the chance of—"

"Yes, Mother," Meg interrupted, bringing her a glass of bourbon. "Genie was a classmate of Lex's at Ashe-Willmott."

"That's all right." She appeared mollified, either by the school's name or the drink.

Phillip entered the room and Meg's mother gave a little gasp of joy, rushing over to him. He kissed her on both cheeks. "Good to have you here, Mother."

"Do you realize how long it's been?"

"Three months?" Phillip ventured.

"Four!" answered his mother-in-law triumphantly. She adored Phillip almost as much as Pel, and sometimes wondered—aloud to Meg—what had moved him to marry her daughter. He was dynamic and forceful—a man who could take the world on his shoulders and carry it to somewhere else. Rose understood him, she felt, better than his wife did.

Rose Borden had always seen herself as a man's woman. If a man made a mistake or behaved badly, that was simply an oversight—but if a woman did the same, it was stupidity. For the remainder of her stay at Topnotch, she found no time to talk with Genie, though she'd often say to her, "We must have a little chat, you and I, and you can tell me all about life over there."

Pel, on the other hand, managed to be near Genie every time they were all together. He'd even asked to come along with the girls on their hike next morning, but Lex told him firmly that it was a private outing.

The Henry Vandergrieffs and Lucy Carlisle arrived on Christmas Eve. Governor Vandergrieff was a Republican, unique in his traditionally Democratic family. The Vandergrieffs' allegiance—particularly to FDR and the New Deal—had marked them as unusual among people of their wealth and influence. But Democrats they all remained, until Henry, youngest son of John Vandergrieff III and his wife, Selena, reached voting age and registered with the Republican party. In 1958, carried on the nation's wave of support for its Republican president, Dwight D. Eisenhower, Henry had been swept into the governor's seat.

His brothers were now supporting John F. Kennedy for election in November, contributing substantially to his presidential campaign. But, despite political differences, Henry made it a point to get on well with them. He had particular admiration for Phillip, whom he regarded as brilliant and unpredictable, because of the broad range of his interests. Phillip always got things done. Even if his scheme looked harebrained on the face of it (at least to Henry), he could always push it through, implement it, and see that it was managed properly.

Henry's family was more formal than Phillip's. Even the children, Genie observed—twin boys of eight and a girl of ten—had learned to behave as though they were always in the public eye. Their mother, Joy, was distant and absentminded, usually sitting near the fire with a drink in her hand, making conversation with anyone who came into the room, scarcely noticing whom she was talking to. Her sister Lucy was flamboyant and constantly in motion, like a butterfly lost on city pavement. Her fluttering voice moved in a constant stream, to the obvious annoyance of Rose Borden.

"Lucy has problems," Lex confided to Genie in their cabin as they were dressing for dinner. "She's unmarried and terrified of getting old."

"She's very pretty," said Genie, slowly brushing out her hair in front of Lex's mirror.

"You think so? She's had two face lifts, and she's only fifty, I think. No one's supposed to know. She had her first done in Switzerland and they pulled the skin too tight, so she looked like a death mask. Then she had another in South America or the Caribbean someplace."

Genie had never knowingly been with anyone who'd had a face lift. "Could I ask her about it?"

Lex laughed. "You better not. She thinks nobody knows. She'd kill me."

Genie was mystified. "Did she have a deformity?"

"Lucy? She was always a good-looking woman, I think. Yes, sure. There's a picture of her as maid of honor at Uncle Henry's wedding, and she's much better-looking than the bride."

"Then why did she have it?" Genie persisted. Her social-studies teacher had regarded plastic surgery as frivolous. But after months of studying about it, Genie still regarded it as a branch of medicine devoted to changing a life from deformed to normal. But why would a normal—no, an *attractive*—person want to change her looks? To what purpose?

"I told you, she's terribly afraid of getting older, and she doesn't want it to show. Eats all kinds of strange health foods, keeps away from the sun—says it causes wrinkles—and dresses like a kid. But it's a losing battle, since she *is* getting older."

"What's wrong with that?" Genie couldn't wait to get older, or at least look it.

"I think Aunt Lucy wants to make up for fun she didn't have when she was younger. The Carlisles were brought up very strictly. Last year Lucy had a boyfriend who was thirty-two."

"Really?" Genie sat on Lex's bed and took a few drags off her cigarette. "What happened?"

Lex ran her hand slowly along Genie's hair. "Gorgeous. You're gorgeous."

Genie shook her head, displacing Lex's hand. "The boyfriend," she reminded her.

"He ran off in the Jag XKE she bought for him. She's got tons of money. Joy does too—their parents made a killing in paper. My family's so boring, don't you think?"

"You're crazy," Genie said, going toward the wardrobe. "Your family's like a novel or a play—all those characters."

"What do you think of Pel?" Lex asked in a calculatedly casual tone.

"Great."

"Yeah, he really is." Lex leaned back, resting her head on her hands against the wall. "Definitely not a Martian. I think he's got a crush on you."

Genie flushed in spite of herself. "Don't be ridiculous. He's so old! Besides, he's your brother. That makes him like mine."

"Dmitri? Is Pel like him?"

"Not really." She tried to visualize Dmitri, but she couldn't fix his whole face in her mind, only single features, disembodied. His eyebrow moving up in contempt, his beautiful lips curled in irony. The scars on his foot, extending up the leg. The sound of his voice calling her. "Dmitri's shorter, blonder. He's not as outgoing as Pel, but . . ."

"What's wrong?" Lex rushed over as Genie sagged against the wardrobe door.

"I miss him," she said. "Terribly."

Lex turned her around and held her. Homesickness, self-pity, the longing to see her brother again—all overwhelmed Genie as she fought against the desire to weep in Lex's arms. "Lex . . ." she began, and had to stop.

Lex waited, holding her.

"You're all I've got now!" Genie blurted out.

"It's all right," Lex whispered, stroking Genie's head. "It'll be all right, Genie love. You'll see. My family will be your family too, and we'll share Pel as a brother."

On Christmas morning there was a stocking for Genie hanging from the mantelpiece along with the other stockings. The tree sparkled, the fire roared and crackled, carols were playing as they opened presents, played with the children, drank eggnog and hot cider until it was time for Christmas dinner.

Pel seated himself next to Genie. The meal took all afternoon and Genie felt she belonged among the dozen people at the table. She was part of the family, and smiled as she thought of it: part of one of the richest families in America, whose name was practically a synonym for capitalism itself.

At Bernard's, unless she was with Sonya in the kitchen, Genie usually had the sense of intruding, even in her own apartment. His house was a showcase which demanded perfection from whatever was exhibited in it, human or inanimate. But Topnotch felt like home.

"What are you smiling about, pretty Genie?" Pel asked.

"I feel good. Everything's simple here."

"You like the place?" He was smiling at her and in the candlelight his eyes were light brown. They changed colors, she realized, though she couldn't remember them in daylight.

"More than very much. The houses seem to grow out of the woods."

"Yes, I like that too. Topnotch was my father's wedding present to Mother. It's a perfect setting for her, don't you think? Natural, strong . . ."

Genie nodded, realizing that Meg appeared differently to each of her children. Like with her own mother: Dmitri had seen her as an angel.

"Last summer I visited Count Leo Tolstoy's home in Yasnaya Polyana," Pel was saying.

"You were in Russia?" Genie asked in surprise.

"Yes, in Moscow for the American Exhibition. A few of us took a car and driver and went out to see it." Genie smiled at him. The fact that he'd been in her country made her feel closer to him, though she'd never been to Tolstoy's home, or even to Moscow. "I was impressed by the simplicity. His grave, you know, is just a small elevation of earth under the trees. When we were there, the sunlight was coming through the leaves and the mound was dappled with sun and shade. No marker, just grass growing over his remains. I thought it was beautiful." He picked up his fork.

"That's wonderful," she said, as a piece of turkey with gravy jumped as he pronged it and sailed into her lap.

He apologized profusely, dipped his napkin in his water glass, and was about to wipe her skirt, but stopped in modesty and handed the napkin over to her. "I hope it won't stain. Please, let me send it to the cleaners. You think lighter fluid might . . . ?"

"It's okay, Pel," she assured him. Without his clumsiness he would be too intimidating, but with his turkey stains on her skirt, Pel was like someone in her family.

Before they all separated in the evening, going back to their individual cabins, Pel took hold of Genie's hand and led her under the mistletoe. He kissed her lightly, his lips barely brushing hers.

The following day, the governor's family flew back, except for Lucy, who, with little encouragement, had agreed to stay on for the New Year's party.

But in the next days Genie and Lex stayed by themselves. Other visitors were arriving, filling up the cabins. Pel had two friends down from Princeton. The girls ignored the bustle. They slept late, went skiing, sat around the fire talking, and a few times begged provisions from Mary so they could make their own dinner in their little house in the woods.

"This is heaven," Genie decided. Despite their long days together, there was never time enough to talk about everything. Lex told Genie about her debutante season in such full detail that Genie felt she'd been there herself. But usually they talked about their own families. Lex, who had been fascinated by Genie's exotic background, understood now how hard it had been for her friend, and how lonely. Genie, who'd felt that Lex had everything, began to see that despite the warmth and material security surrounding her, Lex had constructed a prison of her own, where she withdrew in self-doubt.

"When everything's given to you, it's tough to force yourself to become someone," Lex told Genie as they were putting on their boots. "Mom had it easier than me. I used to envy people who were born poor, or had parents who beat them, or were orphans." Catching herself in the word, Lex looked up. "Sorry. What I mean is, it seemed everyone else had a chance to find out who they really were."

"But you're such a *person*," protested Genie.

"Am I? Sometimes I think I just give a reasonable imitation of one. C'mon, out to brave the elements."

They were most free then, sliding their skis over the coating of snow that had fallen in the night. Outside, where chickadees bustled among the snowy arms of the leafless hardwoods, each girl could forget everything but the moment, in its still, cold beauty.

But images of Pel came to Genie, even as they skied noiselessly, abreast or one behind the other. Genie knew he was attracted to her—she could sense it. The way he quickly averted his eyes when she looked up and caught him gazing at her; the way he stood next to her when they talked, much closer than he had to. She wished she could spend more time with him, but Lex always had plans for just the two of them alone.

Like Lex, Genie realized, Pel was less self-assured than either of his parents. He often seemed to be voicing a silent apology for himself—and yet he was intelligent, knowledgeable, and warm. He possessed none of the Martian traits that Lex had enumerated in grueling detail. On the contrary, Pel seemed to admire women and look up to them. He'd make a perfect husband, she was thinking. But when Lex's voice came from out of the silent whiteness—"What are you thinking about?"—Genie answered, "Nothing."

She wanted to keep those thoughts to herself, though they were the only ones she kept from Lex.

* * *

On New Year's Eve Genie put on the dress she'd bought in Regent's Park specially for the occasion: a blackwatch wool plaid with a full skirt reaching to her ankles. As she fastened the tight bodice, Genie bent over to scoop up her breasts as high as they would go, so the open neckline, edged with lace, would reveal their swell. The three-inch patent-leather belt made her waist look tiny.

She turned in front of the mirror, examining herself over her left shoulder, then over the right. She was pleased with the effect. Her hair was shining, her skin rosy from exposure to the winter air, and her peach lipstick made her lips look fuller, her teeth very white.

Coming into the room, Lex gave a low wolf whistle. "You're something!"

"You don't look so bad yourself," Genie said, blushing to be caught in the act of admiring herself. In wide black pants and a yellow sweater laced with metallic threads, Lex looked splendid, Genie thought. Maybe "spiffy" was the word. She could never understand Lex's dislike of her own appearance.

"May I escort you?" Lex bowed and held out her bent arm.

"With the greatest pleasure." They walked down the stairs of their cabin like a regal pair, got into their down jackets at the bottom, and raced through the cold to the main house.

The band was playing, the musicians in their black tails providing a note of incongruity in a room that resembled a ski hut more closely than a ballroom. The dancers were dressed however they pleased, in tweeds or satins, a few men in tuxedos, others in turtleneck sweaters without jackets.

The buffet table was decked with equal variety: vintage champagne in ice buckets, beer on draft, smoked salmon and caviar placed among the cheeses and cold cuts.

Genie had no time to eat. She was invited to dance as soon as she came in, and from then on she never stopped, as Pel, Phillip, and their friends cut in on her, and she was passed from partner to partner, dancing with the lightness she felt, twirling in the waltzes, dipping in the tangos, spinning out and pirouetting back, told by each man that she was the best dancer in the room. She felt like Cinderella, beautiful as a princess in her first long dress, with its tiny waist, its revealing neckline.

When the music stopped, between numbers, Pel brought her a glass of champagne. She was flushed and glowing, her eyes sparkled, and a few wisps of hair lay in damp tendrils on her forehead and neck. "You're ravishing," Pel said, so close to her that she felt his breath on her face. "I didn't know you were a ballerina—from the Bolshoi or Kirov?"

Genie laughed. The bubbles tickled the end of her nose and made her sneeze. If teacher Kondrashin could see her now! she thought. For an instant she became subdued, but only for an instant. The champagne was tickling her, Pel's eyes hung on her mouth, but he was laughing, too, as she told him about being expelled from ballet class as a baby elephant.

Then the music started again and she was dancing in the arms of a curly-haired young man who was telling her that they'd met before, in his dreams, and that she must come on his family's yacht, down to Rio with him; and before she could answer, Pel was standing there, coming between her and the curly-haired man, telling him, "It's about that time now and I want to have my girl in my arms."

She went into them, but just then the music stopped and all the dancers released each other as they began calling out numbers, counting backward from ten. Pel's arm was around Genie's waist. "Four . . . three . . . two . . ." and then she heard jubilant shouts and the room was plunged into darkness as people called out "Happy New Year!"

Pel was pulling her close against him and Genie raised her face and his lips found hers and their lips pressed against each other. Genie was floating again, she felt she was spinning, as the kiss twirled through her body and his lips pressed more strongly against hers, spreading them apart, their mouths glued together around the O between them, and then she felt his tongue entering her mouth and she jerked away from him as the lights came on and the band started playing again, and people were singing, "Should old acquaintance be forgot . . ."

And in the light he was looking down at her, grinning awkwardly, his hand clasping hers, and he said, "Happy New Year, Genie. Happy new decade." He bent and whispered in her ear, "This is the beginning of us."

9

Each member of the graduating class was requested—required, really—to have "a little private chat" with Miss Willmott about the future. Sitting at the edge of the plush armchair with its white antimacassar, Genie was trying to retain her composure.

"You have a brilliant mind, my dear. You must follow it like a beacon," the headmistress said, a faint smile revealing the pleasure her remarks gave her. Victoria Willmott was accustomed to casting her words rather than simply uttering them. "I congratulate you on your acceptance to Radcliffe."

"Thank you," Genie said meekly. Miss Willmott made her think of a tin soldier. Blood, and life, had long ago been drained from her.

"Do you have any plans, Eugenia? Have you thought about what you intend to study?"

"Medicine," Genie mumbled.

"Oh?"

The condescension she heard in that tiny syllable made Genie add assertively: "Surgery. I plan to go to medical school and become a plastic surgeon."

"Really! I believe you are the first of my girls to come up with such an extraordinary career. It is not well-advised. Obstetrics or pediatrics would be a more reasonable choice."

Genie held her silence and recrossed her ankles.

"In this country," Miss Willmott explained laboriously, "it isn't usual for women to go into medicine, though some do, to be sure, and excel in it. But plastic surgery has no female practitioners, as far as I know. An Ashe-Willmott girl can do better than to engage herself in changing people's looks."

The headmistress smiled. "You have an excellent head on your shoulders, my dear, but let us hope you will not be unduly influenced by appearance. Leave vanity to the vain."

"But—"

Miss Willmott folded her hands. "People should keep the faces God gave them," she pronounced.

"But if 'God' lets babies be born with malformations, or if 'God' allows war to disfigure people, don't you think someone should help them?" Genie asked with passion.

Miss Willmott touched the tip of her tongue to her teeth. She made a steeple of her fingers. "I see." Her voice was steel when she said, "If you intend to involve yourself in such gruesome matters, it's up to you. Perhaps you will consider my advice and come to a more reasoned choice of a career."

"Thank you, Miss Willmott." Genie rose from her chair and, meeting the woman's gaze, walked out of the office without shaking hands.

At the dorm, she dashed off a letter to Lex: "The old witch. Forty years devoted to 'women's education' and all she basically cares about is turning out good housewives. In Russia, most doctors are women. But old Miss Will-not says plastic surgery is 'not well-advised.' Neither is she—ignorant as an old cow."

But Genie's courage in the face of her headmistress had been partly bolstered by the knowledge that there was nothing Miss Willmott could do, one week before commencement, to prevent Genie from graduating as Class Valedictorian.

Bernard basked in the compliments he received on Genie's behalf, keeping his arm on her shoulder as they walked over the grounds after the ceremony. "Well done!" he told her, smiling broadly. "You did me proud, Genia."

"I'm called Genie now," she reminded him once again. His praise, she felt, was for himself, at having bet on a winner.

She entered his new Bentley still wearing her cap and gown. The back ledge of the car was piled high with the flowers Pel had sent, an arrangement of orchids and lady's slippers in subtle and unusual colors: greens, browns, ivory, and black-purple.

"Your admirer has a bizarre taste in flowers," Bernard observed as Ross started the car.

"Why don't you like the Vandergrieffs?" she retorted.

"Like? That has nothing to do with it. We're just not the same kind of people."

They were driving through the campus. For the last time—Genie turned to watch the familiar buildings, the trees and shrubbery, fade into the distance. She remembered clearly the first time she'd ridden up, with Ross. She remembered her fear, her first meeting with Miss Willmott, the terrible girl who'd shown her to her dorm. Her English had still been flawed then, and she'd been so miserable and friendless the first weeks that she hadn't cared if she lived or died.

Lex had changed all that. Craning her neck for the last glimpse, Genie felt only a mild sadness at leaving school behind. It was the easiest of all separations she'd known. Probably, she thought, as she turned and faced forward, it was because, for the first time, she'd completed something before ending it. After final exams, she'd felt she was already on her way to the next step; the last few days at school had felt like anticlimax.

The next step. Radcliffe—four years of college if she remained in America. "Bernard?" she asked.

"What is it, dear girl?"

She faced him, and hesitated. He would go on supporting her, she knew, would continue to ensure she had everything she needed, every material item she desired, and the finest education money could buy. "Why are you my guardian?"

"What do you mean?"

"I mean, why did you *agree* to become my guardian?"

"Your father asked me to," he answered smoothly.

"That's all? He asked you to take care of me for the rest of my life, and you agreed?"

"Not the rest of your life," Bernard said, frowning. "You know better than that. We all thought his exile would be temporary."

"I know," she said impatiently, still trying to forge the words out of the huge unformed question that had been biding its time over nearly two years, waiting to be asked. "But I'm trying to find out why you did it."

"I told you already." His voice was cold.

"Because he asked you to," she mimicked. "That's all? Didn't you get anything in return?"

"That's enough, Genie! You're being tiresome, my dear. The honors you received today have gone to your head. You know as much as there is to know."

"As much as I'm supposed to know, you mean."

"Enough, I said!"

Genie was frightened by her own audacity, and by the new intuitions it brought her. She realized she wasn't able to frame the question because she was afraid of getting his answer—or of not getting it.

Two months before Genie's graduation Bernard had finally become the owner of the most valuable Russian ikon in the world: the Kiev Virgin.

She arrived with a slight pockmark on her left cheek, a touch of skin trouble caused by inadequate padding or rough handling. Bernard found it charming, the small blemish she'd sustained in her arduous journey, like a beauty mark she'd placed there especially for him.

He was overjoyed by her, and rushed home from the office every evening to unveil her in the privacy of his locked library. Beautiful and young, burgeoning with the promise of her son. Her black eyes, unlike the eyes of other Virgins, were not held down in modesty but looked directly at him, and the hint of a smile on her lips kept changing as he looked at her. Sometimes she was serene, but other times she seemed to be mocking him for all his deals and companies, his manipulations of power which were as nothing compared to what she would do by giving birth.

She became his private shrine, and he worshiped her every evening, not as the soon-to-be Mother of God, but as his own Lady, who saw deep into his soul and teased him, flirted with him, encouraged him in her understanding. She was his, he hers: the possessor possessed. No other piece in his collection had ever given him such joy.

He was aware that Genie had been the instrument by which he'd acquired the ikon, and he took new interest in her. He resolved to spend more time with her, make up for his absence from her over the past years, shower her with his favors.

Her willfulness—ingratitude, as he saw it—on the ride home from Ashe-Willmott had disappointed him, but next day